One Night

BOYFRIEND

L. MOONE

CONTENTS

CHAPTER ONE

It takes me a few minutes, bag in one hand, phone in the other, to make my way through the crowded train and towards my seat. I was stressed and cranky anyway. On top of that, I had to make a run for it through the rain and got my hair, as well as mostly everything else, all wet. Bloody London weather. It's bound to be even worse in Edinburgh.

Still, I try to remain calm as I make my way through the rows of occupied seats in my compartment. Irina's invitation took me by surprise, and I'm not entirely sure how to feel about it yet. I couldn't blow her off, but I really didn't feel like going either. She's engaged. How the hell did that happen all of a sudden? Sure, I retreated from everyone in my social circle while trying to pick up the pieces of my life lately, but it's only been six months!

It's difficult not to be cynical, when all you've seen of love is how it can all go to hell in an instant. I wonder how long Irina's engagement is going to last?

She's always been a hopeless romantic, much like myself. Until life taught me not to be.

I'm about to reach my row, when I see someone already sitting there. Spurred on by a determination to fight for my reservation if I have to, I square up with my hands on my hip.

Just when I'm about to voice my complaint, I notice that actually, the rather large man that's already sitting there is in the seat beside mine. And what I assume to be his duffel bag is occupying my space. I take a deep breath, and try to be as composed as possible.

"Mind if I put this up?" I ask him. "This is my spot."

"Oh," he mumbles, while giving me a sheepish look. "I'm so sorry."

He scoots forward and tries to get up, but it's proving difficult. He's so tall, his knees touch the seat in front, and the armrest is digging into his broad frame. What kind of contortionist move did it take for him to get in there in the first place? Watching him struggle stops my irritation dead in its tracks.

"Relax. I've got it. Nothing fragile in here, I hope?" I tentatively lift up the bag. Not nearly as heavy as it looks.

He shakes his head.

I stow it into the luggage rack overhead and shove my much heavier little suitcase in next to it.

Then, I take my time observing the man—my seat neighbor—from the corner of my eye. He's not paying me any attention while I take off my wet coat and put it up there in between the bags; he's too busy trying to adjust the armrest to find a more comfortable position. Maybe he should have bought two seats for himself; he would have had more space. At least he could have sat with his legs spread out so his knees don't touch the seat ahead of him.

But hey. That's hardly my problem now. I'm not giving up my spot, no matter what. I deposit my phone in the little net attached to the chair in front of me and take a seat, while covertly eyeing him up and down once more.

Late twenties or early thirties, a full head of strawberry blond hair and a beard that wouldn't be out of place on the set of *Vikings*. He has a pleasant face, despite or perhaps because of the softness around his jaw and cheeks.

He's *big*, in every possible way. He's wearing some baggy jeans and a black long sleeve t-shirt that's just slightly tight around the waist while he's sitting down. Something in his mannerisms and the way he's avoiding my gaze tells me he's not used to company. Like he doesn't want to be here, but he hasn't got a choice.

That makes two of us, buddy.

My wry observations about the tight spot he's

finding himself in are wearing a little thinner. Not enough to try and find myself another one, but… It's not his fault they make these seats too tight for taller people like him. He's a literal giant! And trains don't give you the option to opt for extra leg room like planes do.

"We could fold that up, if you want." I point at the arm rest that's causing him so much trouble.

He glances in my direction. "Are you sure?"

I force a smile at him and nod. I'll still have my seat, and feel a little less guilty about causing him discomfort. That's already a win. Plus, I could think of worse ways of spending my three hour train ride than sitting next to a larger than life Highlander teddy bear. Assuming he isn't a creep.

A girl can dream, right? Even one who has been properly burned before.

He tugs at the armrest but isn't getting anywhere with it, so I gesture at him to lean over to the other side, allowing me to fold it up. His thigh immediately ends up partially in my leg room once he gets space to spread out.

He smells so nice. Lord have mercy.

I take a seat next to him and pretend not to pay too much attention to his thick leg, which is now resting against mine. Or his arm, which encroached onto my side far enough I could conveniently have a nap on his shoulder in this position. He's so warm.

Or I'm so cold; I don't know which. Either way, it puts my whole body on edge. It's been a while since I've found myself in such close proximity to a guy, and for very good reason.

"I'm sorry," he mumbles, while trying to shift further to his side.

"I'm okay if you're okay," I tell him, while folding my arms to keep us from touching too much. It's rather hopeless, though. "Got a long way to go?"

"All the way to Edinburgh, yeah." He has a hint of a Scottish accent, but may have been living in London long enough to shed most of it.

"Same."

He clears his throat and looks out the window. Or pretends to, because when I glance over at him, our eyes meet in the reflection. Is he checking me out? Or is he just annoyed, because he was hoping this seat would stay empty?

"Well, at least we won't have to get adjusted all over again with any new arrivals along the way, huh?"

"Right."

Okay, that was an awkward thing to say. I should just pop my ear buds in and listen to a podcast or something. Only, my earbuds are in the front pocket of my bag, which is up in the luggage rack. And I'm in no mood to have to get up again.

"Business or pleasure?"

"Huh?" he asks.

God. I'm really no good at small talk.

"Where you're going," I clarify.

"Oh, uh, neither."

Guess he's even worse at making conversation than I am. I pick up my phone and start panic-scrolling. His leg is so warm and inviting. Or perhaps the air in the train is crazy cold, plus I'm all wet because the rain soaked through my coat earlier. That early September downpour I encountered before I reached the station really did a number on me. It didn't help that my umbrella upended and tore in the wind. I find myself relaxing little by little until our arms are touching a little more. God, he's so warm there too, it makes me shiver.

"You, umm..." he starts.

"What?" I turn to face him, only to find him staring at our arms and legs touching. Surely he doesn't have the audacity to tell me to move over, when he's literally the one who's spilling over into my seat!

"You seem cold," he says.

I force myself to breathe calmly again. At this rate, cold is an understatement. If only I'd had the forethought to wear a waterproof jacket. Or packed another warm sweater. Instead, I just had to be stylish and packed not one but two outfits for tomorrow. Ugh.

"It started to pour and then my umbrella folded

over with the wind…" I explain.

"Do you, like–"

Does he ever just finish a sentence on the first attempt? Yeah, he's even worse at peopling than I am, and that's saying something.

"Do you want to borrow a hoodie, or something? I've got one in my bag. At least it'll be dry," he says at last.

I cock my head to the side while looking over at him. Is he trying to make a pass at me? His expression sure as hell doesn't suggest it. It actually looks like he's regretting his question. That means he's genuinely trying to help, bless him.

Could it be? Have I encountered the rarest of breeds in the wild; a genuinely nice guy?

"Aw, that's so sweet! I think I'll be fine, though," I say, while rubbing my icy hands together and blowing into them. That only makes me shiver more, though. "Surely they'll crank up the heat once we start moving."

He sighs. "Yeah, I'm afraid the heating is out. We had an announcement about it just before you got on."

"Fuck." Lucky me; I booked a seat on Freezer Express. At this rate, I'll definitely catch a cold by the time I get to Edinburgh. That's going to be fun. Sniffling and sneezing my way through tomorrow's fancy dinner. I might as well cancel right now.

"In that case, I'm going to accept your offer after all, if you don't mind."

"Be my guest." He awkwardly gestures up at the luggage rack, which he obviously has no hope of reaching with me still in my seat. I guess I'm getting up. And if I'm up, I might as well get the bag down myself.

I hand it to him, and watch as he digs around in it. He hands me a humongous hooded sweatshirt with one hand, and his substantially emptier backpack with the other.

I swiftly put it back in the rack. Then, I take a seat with the hoodie in my lap and try to get out of my clingy wet sweater. It's a struggle, and I'm in real danger of flashing this stranger along with the rest of the train carriage.

"Umm... If it's not too weird, can you hold on to the bottom of my t-shirt for me? Everything's so wet, it's sticking," I tell him, while gesturing down at myself.

His brow furrows in tense concentration as he carefully holds on to the hem of my top, and I finally manage to wiggle out of my sweater. The t-shirt I'm left with is a bit low cut; more so now that it's clinging to my bra. You can see *everything* right through the thin fabric, down to the exact floral pattern of the lace trim that surrounds the cups.

I follow his gaze down into my cleavage, where it

lingers briefly, before he looks up at me. He's blushing, which turns my annoyance into amusement. He seems completely out of his comfort zone. It's kind of endearing. I've had my fill of players for this year already.

"I'm sorry," he mumbles.

"Entirely my fault for putting the girls on display," I say.

He's trying really fucking hard not to look again. Little beads of sweat appear just along his hairline. God, it's actually adorable. And I'd be lying if I didn't appreciate the attention at least a little. Mainly because he doesn't strike me as the sort of guy who would ever actually *try* anything. He can barely get through a complete sentence before losing his nerve!

I quickly get up, pop my wet sweater up on the luggage rack, then put on his hooded sweatshirt. It's so big, it drapes halfway down my thighs. I wrap myself up in it tightly and sit back down. "That's so much better, thank you. Umm... What's your name, anyway?"

"Chris."

"Thank you. You're a lifesaver, Chris. I'm Violet." I stretch out my hand and find myself shivering all over again when his great big warm hand grasps mine before giving it a singular shake.

He withdraws much too soon, and clears his throat while fixing his gaze on the window again. Our train has started moving, leaving London St. Pancras behind. I look at it too for a moment, then wrap my arms around myself and snuggle into the sweatshirt. It's so soft and inviting. A bit like him, I guess. It's got a fluffy liner in it, which is just perfect for my current condition. And it smells just as nice as the rest of him does. Finally, I can feel the tension in my shoulders fade.

CHAPTER TWO

*** Violet ***

"I'm going to a funeral, actually," Chris says, jerking me out of my moment of Zen. I think I very nearly dozed off just there. "You asked: business or pleasure."

"Oh shit, I'm so sorry. Are you okay?" I ask.

He shrugs. "We weren't close. At least not lately."

The silence between us has become loaded now. Do I ask the obvious question? He mentioned the funeral first. That suggests he wants to talk about it. I glance in his direction. The color has faded from his cheeks again, and he's twitching his leg—the further one from me—rather tensely.

"Whose funeral? If you're comfortable telling me..."

I don't know what I'm expecting in terms of an answer. It's fifty-fifty between being told to mind my own damn business or a grandparent, considering he looks just a few years older than me.

"My dad."

That's not... Fuck. I'm so flustered, I instinctively

reach out for him and put my hand on his knee. That's weird, right? I mean... I don't know him. But seeing as I'm already pressed up against his leg and wearing his clothes, we're well beyond weird already.

"I'm so sorry, hey," I stammer.

In the window, I see his expression twist as he tenses his jaw. He's so not okay, no matter what he says. Now I know why he's on this train, looking like he'd literally rather be anywhere else. And I thought I was having a hard time lately! Crap, it breaks my heart.

I wish I could say something to help. But, what? We've only just met. Who the hell am I to offer words of comfort to a total stranger!

"Want to talk about it?" I ask finally.

He shrugs. "What's it matter? Not going to bring him back, is it?"

I shake my head. "No. It sure won't."

Wow. This is going to be an awkward four hours at this rate. Open mouth, insert foot, indeed.

"I'm just so fucking angry, you know?" he says after a brief pause.

"Yeah..." I mumble, though I'm not sure what he means.

I turn my hand palm up and wait. He grabs it, almost on autopilot. Jesus, still so warm. I stare down at it, and at how his t-shirt sleeve has shifted slightly, revealing part of a strange round scar.

"You're resentful that he's gone?" I wonder aloud. Then again, he said they weren't close. Maybe there was unfinished business between them.

"When I was little, he and I would go get lunch. Or we'd catch a game at home. Once he took me camping in the Highlands, but that was a long time ago."

"Sounds nice."

Chris scoffs. "If he was so nice, then why didn't he keep me safe, huh?"

My heart is racing now. Shit, did he used to hurt him? Is that what that scar is about? It looks pretty old. I try to sneak a better look at it while squeezing his hand.

"Then why did he let her get away with everything she did?"

"Chris... I'm really sorry," I tell him, though I'm still not entirely sure what we're talking about.

He turns to me with tears in his eyes. This poor guy is having the worst time. Something tells me I'm the only person he's opened up to about this. Awkward as this conversation is, I'm also glad to be of help. He seems like a good person. He's going through so much and his first instinct after I sat down next to him was to offer me something to wear because I was freezing. Even if he looked damn nervous asking me, or probably because of it. That's a heart of gold, right there. Maybe my instincts about men aren't as bad as I thought.

"I know it must sound hollow and stupid right now, but it will get better… eventually," I tell him, while fighting the tears welling up in my own eyes.

He glances at me and inhales sharply through his teeth. "Fuck, now I've made you cry. I'm just going to shut up."

I shake my head. "No, no. It's fine. Don't worry about me. We can talk for as long as you want. At least for the next four hours and however many minutes, 'til we get where we're going." I force a smile.

He presses his lips together and nods briefly. "Thanks."

"Thanks for the sweatshirt. I totally owe you for that." I squeeze his hand again. He squeezes back. That little gesture warms me from the inside out.

"Forget it. You can keep it."

"When is it; the funeral?" I ask.

"Tomorrow morning."

"You'll be okay. You can vent to me now, so that you can go there with your head held high, okay? Fuck whoever hurt you. They're not worth shit and they can't do it anymore."

His bottom lip trembles. He sniffles loudly and shakes his head.

"Everyone will be on my case to move back home now that she's on her own."

"Your mom?" I wonder aloud.

He closes his eyes and his expression tenses. Was she the one who hurt him when he was a child? And his dad let it happen? That's really fucked up. No way should he move back in with his childhood abuser. But then, who the hell am I to tell him what to do?

"She's always had a temper. With Dad too. And he always just let it happen. And then he'd take me for fried chicken afterwards."

"That hardly makes it okay."

"Right? And I never got to ask why he didn't—why he didn't stop it? Or, why he never left her, got me out of there. When I was finally old enough to leave on my own, I was so pissed off I didn't speak to either of them. Not for the last ten years."

"Can't blame you, but now it's too late," I conclude. No wonder he's messed up about it. He's not getting any closure now, at least not from his dad. He must have so many unanswered questions.

"What about..." I take a deep breath, swallowing the worry that I'm about to hugely overstep. "What about confronting her about how she treated both of you? It's no use keeping her secrets anymore," I ask.

He stares at me for a moment. There's a range of emotions written on his face. Shock, fear, maybe. But mostly a hefty dose of frustration, probably at me for suggesting shit I don't know anything about. Which is fair.

"I don't think I could. She had everyone else fooled. The rest of my family has been after me to patch things up. And I've been ignoring all of their messages for years." He shrugs and shakes his head.

"But you know better. And your dad knew better too, but he can't speak for himself anymore."

"You don't know how she can be. She will know exactly the thing to say to shut me up. And there's tons of material for her to work with."

"You can't move back in with that woman, though," I say.

He stares at me blankly. "I guess he did always act like a buffer. Without him there... I don't know how I'll face her."

"What if..." I bite my bottom lip. I'm about to say something even stupider. Something I might regret immediately, because it'll sound so ludicrous. Still, at least it'll give me something to do to take my mind off of my own issues. "What if I tag along? I'll be your buffer. A neutral party."

He opens his mouth, then closes it again before finally voicing his protest. "You cannot be serious!"

I make a face. "I know, this sounds wild. And I'm not a big fan of funerals, I mean, who is, right? But... I just really want to help."

"No way. That's... That's..."

I look down at our hands, still clinging onto each other for dear life. Me and my big mouth. I don't like meeting people's families when they're nice, and I want to walk into that snake pit voluntarily? For some guy I just met twenty minutes ago? Why? All because he let me wear his sweater?

Am I really that easy? Or that starved for male attention? Am I really dreading Irina's engagement party that much, that I'd literally rather attend a stranger's funeral?

"How would I even explain your presence?" he mumbles.

"Oh that's the easiest part. You'd tell them I'm your girlfriend, obviously," I blurt out.

He stares at me. It's so awkward, I can't help but avert my gaze. Me and my big fucking mouth. Then he lets out a chuckle and shakes his head.

"Literally nobody would buy that."

"Why? Are you gay?" I ask.

That makes him laugh out loud. Well, at least laughter is better than tears.

"No, but..."

"Then? Not your type?" I pry.

"I don't exactly—I don't have a type."

"Bullshit. Everyone has a type," I say.

"In that case, everyone will plainly see that I'm not your type," he says. "Most of all, Mom. She'll see right through us and it'll all go to hell from there."

I glance over at him and purse my lips. "You could be, you know? My type."

"I don't buy it."

"You don't know me well enough to know my type," I argue.

"Good point. I don't know you at all. But I know me."

"Oh yeah? Enlighten me." I don't even know why I'm arguing so hard. I guess I don't like it when people make assumptions about me.

His eyes narrow as he looks at me. I guess he's done laughing and is instead getting annoyed with me now.

"I'm nobody's type, okay? I'm a comic book nerd who spends too much of his spare time playing video games. This is probably the longest conversation I've ever had with a girl."

"I like comic books and video games just fine," I counter. Well, some video games at least. Comic books? I enjoyed some of the Marvel movies... Does that count?

"You don't mean it. You're just being nice because you're stuck in the seat next to mine," he grumbles.

I shrug and look him up and down once. "Okay, here's the deal. I said you *could* be my type. With a few tweaks. The potential is very much there."

"I'm not fucking Cinderella and we don't have time to get me ready for the ball, okay?" he snaps.

That's too much. I squeeze my lips together tightly, but I can't stop myself from giggling.

"What?" His expression is a mixture of exasperation and surprise.

"That's fucking hilarious, Chris. Oh my god!" I wheeze, in between fits of laughter.

"Wasn't meant to be, but okay."

It takes me a minute to recover from my outburst. A minute during which I note that we're still holding hands. It's starting to feel natural, even. It's not just warming my hand, it's making me feel warm and fuzzy deep inside my chest. What a sucker I am.

Once I calm down fully, I allow myself to really look at him some more. At his hair, which could stand to see a brush or comb, maybe some conditioner. And his beard, which is just a bit too wild to be entirely fashionable. I wasn't exaggerating, the basics are very much there.

And the confused blue eyes staring at me; shit, those are most definitely already there.

Then there's the clothes. Can't argue with simple jeans and t-shirts. Maybe a nice shirt to go over the top, folded a few times at the sleeves to reveal those thick forearms of his... A sprinkling of chunky jewelry, a decent watch...

Okay, so he's a bit chubby, and that might be a deal breaker for some women, but not me. The fact that he's so damn awkward around women definitely makes him my type, I've decided right now. The opposite has been a fucking nightmare for me. I kind of like the challenge of having to go after a guy for a change. Maybe a man like him would actually be loyal and not chase after whoever else seems convenient at the time.

"We'd need to go shopping. Where are you staying?" I ask.

He shakes his head, confused. "I was going to go straight home."

"Oh no. We're not ready for that. Much too soon. In that case, you're coming with me to my Airbnb. Tell your family there's been some delay and you're arriving in the morning. That way we have time to get used to each other. Make it more convincing for tomorrow."

"Get used to each other? Are you bloody hearing yourself?"

"Well, do you have a better plan?" I ask.

"Plan? No, I don't have a fucking plan for my dad's fucking funeral!" he rants. If he's trying to intimidate me and put me off with his tone, it's not working. If anything, it's making me more steadfast.

"I do. I've already got a to-do list right here." I tap my index finger to the side of my temple to make my point. "We can do this, Chris!"

He stares at me for a few seconds, stunned. "Why? Why do you want to get involved at all?" he asks finally.

A fair question, which I'm not sure I have a proper

answer to. "I want to help you. Sounds like it's about time someone did that. Plus, I totally owe you for not letting me freeze to death on this train."

His expression falls again. I've hit a nerve, though I didn't mean to. It's the right answer though, in hindsight, so I double down.

"Chris... You seem like you're one of the good guys. Isn't it time you caught a break?" I ask, softly. Sweetly.

"I..." He looks so damn lost now, I wonder if I've pushed things too far.

"You don't worry about anything now, okay? Everything will work itself out; you'll see." I squeeze his hand yet again, and even though he's staring out the window again, like clockwork, he squeezes it right back.

CHAPTER THREE

*** Chris ***

The train ride so far has passed in a blur. I don't even know much time has elapsed; I've been so shell shocked by Violet's suggestion that I could hardly focus on much else. The drab, rainy countryside zips past at a dizzying pace, and I am trying my damndest to calm the thoughts racing in my mind.

I glance over at her—Violet—in the reflection in the window. She's pushy. So pushy, that while she carried on arguing with me, I forgot why I didn't just go with it.

She wants to help, she says. That's rather sweet, even if I'm unsure of her motivation. And I don't want to face Mother alone; I really don't. I've been haunted by the prospect of it. That's why I poured my heart out to her earlier. I couldn't contain it any longer.

As much as I thought I was over it… Ever since the news came, I barely slept a wink, because all that old shit kept rushing back at me every time I closed my eyes.

All those memories.

I rub the cigarette burns on my arm. They're underneath my sleeve and have been healed for years, and yet they still sting like it all happened yesterday. All of my scars do.

The moment I took my seat on this train, I was consumed by a sense of doom like I was traveling not to Dad's funeral, but my own. Like everything I had done to try and get over it all was for nothing, and I was going to end up just like him. As soon as she'd get her claws into me again, I'd be stuck in that house forever.

She'd outlive me too, I'm certain of it. Because I'd go down the same road he went down. I'd eat and drink and pop pills to forget. But it all takes a toll and I got a headstart on all of it.

At eleven I was big enough to pass for seventeen. Made it easier to buy beer at the supermarket, which got me set on my own path of self destruction before I ever even finished school. I tried to get things under control for the past ten years, and I almost managed it too. The news of his death had me slipping again.

Violet doesn't know any of that. She thinks I'm just a guy with a mean mom and a dead dad. She thinks she can take me shopping and *get used to me*— whatever that means—and convincingly pretend to be a couple tomorrow. But she doesn't have a clue who I really am. And where I came from.

There is nothing but darkness here. Whereas she's all light. How could she know? She has no idea what people are capable of. What they do to themselves to cope. A part of me feels envious of that, but an even bigger part is glad for her. It's a *good*thing that she doesn't know. To grow up shielded from all of this shit truly is a gift.

"Okay, so if we're going to pass as a couple, we have to work quickly," Violet says, snapping me out of my thoughts. "Favorite things. Music, movies, games, books, whatever. Go!"

I stare at her for a moment, unable to form the words. "You're serious, huh?"

"Dead serious. Excuse the turn of phrase." She looks away awkwardly, but she never lets go of my hand. It was weird at first, to touch her, but it's starting to get easier. I'm almost dreading the moment I'll have to let go. The first girl to ever hold my hand. That's pathetic. Still, I kind of love her for it. Her assertiveness is a breath of fresh air, simply because it's so alien to me.

"Uhh... Well, I'm rather partial to Brandon Sanderson's books... Videogames; mostly *Call of Duty* and *World of Warcraft*. Music... You probably wouldn't have heard of anything I tend to listen to."

"Try me."

I wrack my brain for some reference that's at least a little mainstream. "Okay, so you know Jack Black, the actor? He's actually got a band too."

She's grinning at me. "Tenacious D, huh? I can get on board with that."

"No way... You didn't strike me as that kind of girl." I mentally go through some of the more explicit song lyrics in my head. Surely not!

"Do I dare ask what kind of girl I did strike you as?" She eyes me suspiciously. Now that she's wrapped up from head to toe in my faded black sweatshirt and her eye makeup is smudged from the rain, I maybe *could* see her as a bit of an emo girl after all.

"You were wearing a baby pink sweater just now. Just saying. I figured you might be into K-Pop or whatever the latest flavor of boy band is."

She bursts out laughing. "That's cute. *You're* cute, you know that? So wrong, but very cute."

I've certainly never been referred to as 'cute' before. And if she wasn't looking at me with such a big, bright grin on her face right now, I might have wondered if she's making fun of me. That smile. Bloody hell. That smile of hers could start wars and topple civilizations. I need to figure out how to make her do it again and again.

"Uhm. Well, what about your favorites, then?" I ask.

Her grin turns into a subtle smile and her eyes go dreamy. "Umm so, I like System of a Down and the

Offspring. Sometimes a little bit of Nirvana. And actually I've been meaning to read some of Brandon Sanderson's stuff, but haven't had the time, between work and all. Maybe you can let me know where to start?"

"Uhh, sure thing..." She's joking, right? She's trying to manufacture some overlap in our tastes because she can sense that I still think her plan isn't going to work. But why is she so invested in this?

"But yeah, my favorite color is pink, and I love unicorns, so I guess that kind of stands out."

Pink and unicorns. Got it. "What's your favorite food?" I ask.

"Pizza, obviously." She shrugs like it was a dumb question.

I smile and shake my head. "Obviously, huh?"

"Yep. Yours?"

I let out a sad chuckle, but don't immediately answer. Everything. All the food. Except, I hate it too. My relationship with food has always been a complicated one.

"In that case, I'm going to assume it's pizza as well, because that's the correct answer," she says.

Okay, I mouth.

"And to celebrate how compatible our tastes are, we're going to get the absolute best takeaway pizza in Edinburgh tonight. It's right around the corner from where I'm staying— where *we're* staying," she adds. "I promise, you'll love it."

Her tone leaves no room for disagreement. Not that I'd dream of refusing her anything. How could I? She deserves to get whatever her heart desires…

"Are you getting warmer now?" I ask, looking down at our hands which still cling to each other on top of my knee. Is the skin under her fingernails supposed to be purplish blue?

"Getting there, yeah. The hoodie is helping." She looks up at me through her clumpy wet lashes. It makes my heart race and my palms clammy. She reaches for my other hand, which had been picking at the scars on my arm. Shit, she's still so cold. I take both her hands in between mine and try to massage some warmth into them.

She just watches, which in turn makes me stop, awkwardly.

"I'm sorry," I mumble.

"For?"

"I... I'm sorry if this is inappropriate."

"I'm your girlfriend, remember? It would be weirder not to." The way she says it makes the hairs on my arms stand up and my throat close up. Jesus Christ. All the while, my mind is screaming at me. *Don't fall for it! She's nothing of the sort! This is a trap!*

"You're nuts," I stammer.

"Okay, well, technically we've only covered a bit of small talk so far. That's hardly enough to convince anyone. Time for some real talk, okay?" she says.

"Mhm."

"Best and worst days of your life and why," she says.

My mind is racing with potential responses. All of them fit into the latter category. I let go of her hands and wipe my palms on my legs to get them to stop sweating. It doesn't work. Simultaneously, my chest gets tight, which is making me struggle for air.

"Hey!" she whispers, while reaching for my face and guiding it in her direction until our eyes meet. "I'm sorry. You don't have to answer if you don't want to."

Her expression is tender, caring. That's something I've only ever seen in movies. Or in my dreams. Certainly no one has ever looked at *me* like this. Nevermind a pretty girl like her. And the longer I stare into those big, concerned gray eyes of hers, the more I want to answer her questions to the best of my ability.

"When I moved into my own place, five years ago. That was the best day," I say.

She smiles, which is just *everything*. But as much as I want to fulfill the assignment she has set, I just can't bring myself to.

"There are too many worst days to count," I say, finally. "You?"

She presses her lips together and takes a deep

breath, holding it for a few seconds before starting to talk. "My best day... When I got my first proper order after starting my own business. I paint murals for a living; it's been a couple years since I've been able to focus on that full time."

"Wow, that's impressive!" I smile at her, but she doesn't reciprocate.

"Worst day... When I found my ex-boyfriend in bed with one of my best friends. Two people I cared most about in the world; I lost them both in one go."

This time it's she who breaks eye contact. In fact, she seems to wilt right in front of my eyes. My chest swells with anger. How could anyone do that to her?

I don't know what comes over me, but instead of taking her hand again, I put my arm around her and pull her against me. She doesn't fight it; in fact, she seems to surrender to me almost completely and sighs when the side of her head makes contact with my chest.

"I would never cheat on you," I whisper, while holding her close.

She stirs, which makes me freeze up. Fuck. Did I literally just tell her that? What a dumbass thing to say. We're just pretending to be a couple, after all!

But rather than fight me or pull away, her hand ends up on my upper arm as she hugs me back.

"Me neither," she says.

Bizarre as this whole situation is, I kind of believe

her. All of this now makes sense. I don't know how long ago it happened, but she's obviously still deeply hurt.

This pretend relationship. This whole situation. Maybe it's her way of feeling in control again. I can't blame her. I guess it wasn't just me who needed help. She needs something too; hopefully I'll be able to give it to her before we inevitably part ways again.

My hand ends up in her hair, caressing her softly. She shivers a little, which just makes me hug her tighter. Although she said she'd started to warm up, I can feel evidence to the contrary radiate through the hoodie and into me. She's freezing still. If only she'd said something, we could have done this sooner.

I rub her back, which seems to make her relax into our hug even more. Her face is now hidden in my chest, which should be weird and awkward, but actually feels strangely natural. And her hand... so far it rested on my bicep, but as she melts into me, she tucks it in under my arm, with her palm flat on my side.

I try not to focus on how weird that feels. To have her touch me so intimately. My first hug with a girl, which happened only a short while after my first time holding hands. No matter how many wonderful sensations our continued contact stirs up for me, I try my damndest to keep calm.

"Violet," I say.

"Yeah?"

"Anything you need. I'm here."

She shivers again, and I rub her back some more. But then, much too soon, she pulls away.

Her eyelashes are wet again. And as I look down, I realize that my shirt is too. Poor girl's been crying over the two assholes who betrayed her. Who never even deserved her in the first place.

"I'm supposed to be helping you. Now look at me. Fuck," she complains, with an apologetic smile playing on her lips.

I don't know what to say to that. Hell, I still don't know how we started chatting ever since she sat down next to me. She's been running the show all along. And now she looks so small. And so sad. And my heart is breaking just looking at her. How do I ever fix this?

"Sounds like we could be helping each other instead," I mumble.

She smiles up at me, wraps her hand around the back of my neck, and gives me a peck on the lips. Or it would have been a peck, if she hadn't lingered there for a couple of seconds, absolutely taking my breath away.

"You're the best, Chris," she tells me when withdrawing again.

I'm speechless. My first kiss. How many firsts am I going to experience on this train? And how do I convince my racing heart that this is all just make believe? Come tomorrow, assuming she even follows through on her crazy plan of tagging along to the funeral, this will all be over. I'll never see her again after that.

A relief for her, no doubt. But a motherfucking tragedy for me. Because everything that's happened in the span of this last hour or so has been life changing for me. More so because I totally don't deserve any of it.

CHAPTER FOUR

*** Violet ***

"You're the best, Chris," I tell him. It's all I can manage, but there's so much more that I just can't find the right words to articulate.

He *is* the best. Already the best boyfriend I ever had, and we're only pretending. Probably *because* it's not real. Because real men aren't like this. They aren't this nice.

Real men tell women all they want to hear and then take what they want and move on. Real men will do whatever they will get away with for as long as they can, without hesitation or remorse.

Real men cheat with your best friend.

Then again, when he said he'd never cheat on me, I wanted to believe it. Even if it was just part of our little game. Maybe because he isn't a ladies' man, it sounded a lot more genuine. If I hadn't started a conversation between us, he probably would have ignored me the whole journey. And we both would have missed out on this experience.

Looking at his face, I can tell that it means

something to him too. I can see the changes in him. The confusion. The gentleness in his eyes. The little twitches and erratic breaths, betraying his excitement. Or is it anxiety?

He said he's nobody's type. I thought that was a weird thing to say, but does that mean— Could he really be as inexperienced as that suggests? What have I gotten myself into? The more I stare into his gorgeous blue eyes, the less I feel like looking away again.

When he hugged me, it overwhelmed me. Not just physically, although yes, it did that too. But I felt engulfed in a feeling I never knew before. A sense of safety, of home.

In his arms, I felt at peace. And yet... I also felt restless for *more*.

I look up at his face, tense and conflicted as it is, and I really want to kiss him properly. Would he like that too? Or am I way off base here and getting suckered in by yet another guy who knows just how to play me?

For just a moment, in his arms, I felt a heaviness lift off my chest which I hadn't even realized was there. For a glorious few seconds, I didn't feel so alone. Could he tell? Did he feel it too?

I must be losing my fucking mind. I don't even know this guy. Best case scenario, we go through with the plan and I help him confront his mom and the rest of his family tomorrow. He gets to air his side of the story, maybe get a little closure on all the terrible things that happened to him when he was little... And I... I get to stand by his side. Feel like I've done a good deed, enjoy his company for a little while, and maybe get another one of these hugs.

Isn't that all a girl can hope for?

And maybe by the end of all this, I'll have convinced myself that good men still exist out there just enough to be able to celebrate Irina's engagement with her. Because the way I've felt about it so far would have me drinking too much wine and making snide remarks about how it's not going to last anyway. And that, combined with the fact that I've essentially ignored her for the past 6 months, will ensure that I lose the only friend I have left.

Then why is my heart telling me a whole different story right now? Why is it telling me that we're going to carry on cuddling on this train, then we're going to do the shopping I have half-forgotten about already, get our pizza on the way to the Airbnb, curl up in bed and watch some TV, and...? Not like a one night stand, because that's yuck. But like a one night boyfriend. One night, which I already know I would like to extend indefinitely if given half a chance.

Because that's how my heart works. I fall head over ass, always to my own detriment. I'm too easy. Too eager.

Too desperate.

Especially now. For six months I've been focusing on my business and nothing else. Nobody to confide in. No boyfriend to go on dates with in between projects, or message with late at night. I'm so completely starved for affection and understanding, I'm actually taking a complete stranger home with me. I should be ashamed of myself, only... I'm not.

"Are you okay?" Chris asks.

My god, he's so sweet.

"A lot better now," I say.

We keep staring into each other's eyes. *This is good,* I tell myself. *If we keep doing this, we're totally going to pass as a real couple tomorrow.*

But it's also dangerous. Because how in the hell am I supposed to say goodbye now? How will I ever let go? Then again, that's a problem for tomorrow. And I'm still freezing, and Chris is so warm, I can't help but cuddle up with him again.

So, I try my best to swallow my concerns about where all this is going, and just go with the flow. I put my arm around him again, tucking my hand in nice and warm at his side, and lean my head against his shoulder. And he hugs me back. Then I close my eyes, and I stay right where I am. Listening to his heartbeat, so rushed and urgent, and his hurried breaths, which in turn speed up my own.

And I try my best not to think about all the filthy

wonderful things I'd like to do to him once we're alone...

CHAPTER FIVE

* Chris *

With my arm around Violet, and her head against my chest, the rest of the train journey passes by much too soon. We still chat, but not throughout. I think she dozes off against me a couple of times, though I can't be sure. I certainly couldn't sleep if I wanted to, no matter how exhausted I've been since getting the news.

Her body pressed up into me is too distracting. And the effect she's having on me physically, too shame inducing. This continued closeness is making me want things. Things I would never admit to anyone, nevermind her.

Even when she wakes up shortly before we're due to arrive, I can barely focus on our conversation. Except to realize that we live barely five minutes away from each other. She's got a studio apartment near the quirky coffee shop on Teddington High Street, and I'm in a block of flats a few streets over, closer to the park. In a city as big as London, what are the chances? Is it a sign from the universe? Were we meant to meet on this train today?

It can't be, because we're just playing a game. And it'll be over all too soon. We may end up back in Teddington when this is all over, and we might still never see each other again…

When we pull into our final station, Edinburgh Waverly, she straightens herself fully, and turns to look at me again.

"We're here!"

I can't match her enthusiasm. For my money, I would have preferred to stay exactly how we were. She jumps up, grabs her coat and little suitcase out of the overhead storage rack, then gestures at me to join her. It's a lot more difficult for me. First to get myself up off my ass in the narrow space between my seat and the backrest of the seat in front of me. Especially since my left foot has fallen asleep...

And once I'm up, I have to awkwardly maneuver myself past her empty seat and into the aisle of the train, before getting my backpack down. I can hear the whispers. I can feel the stares.

You're a disgrace, I hear Mother's voice say. *Look at the state of you!*

I awkwardly look down at myself. My t-shirt is weirdly stretched across my chest and belly, exaggerating just how out of shape I am.

Violet's eyes burn into me. My cheeks turn crimson with embarrassment. I can't bring myself to make eye contact with her. Because she's probably regretting every single thing that's happened these past few hours. Surely, the only right way to end this situation is for both of us to go our separate ways and forget all about her stupid plan.

But when I finally dare glance at her face, I see her beaming smile.

"Chris, come on! We have things to do and places to be!" She already has her coat on as she tugs at my hand to get moving. I lift my own bag up onto my right shoulder, and follow her to join the queue of people waiting to exit the train.

She's got a firm grasp on my hand, which is just as well, because if she didn't, I would have lost my nerve and fled. Once we're outside on the platform, she turns to me, gets up on her tippy toes, and puts her hand on my cheek, just for a moment.

"You're so tall, Chris. I feel like I have my very own bodyguard!" she says, smiling again.

Just like that, she's taken my breath away. Again.

I clear my throat. "Okay... Now, where are we going?"

She looks me up and down, which is weird enough to make me want to crawl into a hole and hide. "I think... A visit to the hair salon is in order."

I instinctively reach for my beard and rake my hand through it. "Don't you make me cut it off!"

"Oh I would never! Just a little bit of tidying up."

She grins and gestures with her thumb and index finger. "A tiny little bit."

I don't know how I feel about that. But then again, Violet has already turned away from me and is tugging at my hand to follow her. She's unwilling to negotiate, and frankly, I don't know how I would refuse her anything. And so, I follow her lead. Off the platform, out of the station, and into Edinburgh Old Town. I instinctively take her little suitcase from her and opt to carry it, rather than roll it behind me, since the handle is comically short for me.

We walk for a few minutes. Her, with determined strides towards a set destination, and me... Awkwardly shuffling behind her, up the cobbled streets crowded with tourists and locals alike, wondering just how much further it will be. All the while she's chatting away about how she loved going to university in Edinburgh, and it's so weird to be back because seemingly nothing has changed.

I don't say much. This place doesn't hold many happy memories, so the fact that it still looks the same isn't a plus for me. As far as I'm concerned, my life started in London. Specifically, in the quaint little suburb of Teddington, where I finally managed to get a place of my very own.

Also, I'm not used to walking this much, and the streets aren't very level. Those hours folded into the cramped train seat did a number on my lower back.

I don't recall the last time I voluntarily left the house until this morning for anything other than buying groceries. And I've certainly never been to a fecking hair salon.

But, five minutes later, here we are. The narrow alley we entered isn't inviting at all, but when we push through the door, the shop's interior is surprisingly airy and clean.

"Violet, darling! Aren't you a sight for sore eyes? How long has it been, three years at least?"

I watch as the man with the sharply styled French beard and plucked eyebrows gives Violet a side-hug.

"How have you been? Well, I hope?" he says. "Your hair looks fab, by the way. What can I do for you today?"

"All good, thanks so much, Jase! How about you? I was hoping you could work some of your magic on my date here." She smiles brightly, first at him, then at me.

The hairdresser, Jase, looks me over, a single eyebrow raised, and I wish that the earth would swallow me up. She knows this guy and she introduced me as her date, as if it was the most natural thing in the world. And now, the two of them are standing off to the side, mumbling things about shampoo and hair masks and trimming dead ends like I'm not even part of the equation.

Jase scratches his chin and checks me out again.

"The beard, especially, looks a bit dry... Some deep conditioning is in order."

"Go for it. Just keep the length."

"Oh, it's glorious! Even if you asked me to cut it, I would refuse!" Jase says.

"I know, right?" Violet chirps. "Glorious is exactly right!"

They grin at each other, and I've never felt so out of place in my life. Jase gestures at me to sit down in one of the chairs, which looks about as tight as the train seat was, meaning it's going to be a challenge. But seeing as I don't have a choice, I do as asked, almost expecting the thing to collapse underneath me. Luckily, I'm spared that embarrassment.

Within moments of me sitting down, Jase covers me in one of those big black sheet things, stuffs a rolled up towel behind my neck, and makes the seat recline in his direction. Before I can even say a word, I'm leant back, with my scalp being doused in warm water. I immediately close my eyes and try to relax, but I'm still just so overwhelmed, I don't know what to think.

"Is Linda still around? I think we need a manicure as well," I hear Violet say. What the actual fuck? She didn't think I needed a manicure when we were holding hands for hours earlier!

Jase clicks his tongue and leans in closer to me. "She's a handful, our Violet, I know. But don't worry,

I'll take good care of you. What's your name?"

"Chris."

"Nice to meet you, Chris. I'm Jason, but everyone tends to call me Jase. Where did you two lovebirds meet?"

God, this is so weird. So alien. And I don't know how to answer that. Especially since this is all a big lie.

"On the train, actually," Violet says. "We happened to be sitting next to each other and hit it off immediately."

"That's so romantic; your very own meet cute!" Jason exclaims. "Does he speak actual full sentences too?"

Violet laughs. "You're too much!"

"I'll speak once I have something sensible to say," I grumble.

"Right you are," Jason says, while running his fingers through my wet hair, detangling it. It's strangely relaxing. I open my eyes just in time to watch Violet sit down on one of the other stools and roll it in my direction. She grabs my hand and threads her fingers through mine. That little gesture calms me and gets my heart racing faster all at the same time.

"Jase is the best stylist I know. He's going to do a great job. He's going to get you looking super sharp for tomorrow."

"Aw, thanks, girl!" Jason pipes up behind me.

I want to protest, and to say that none of this is necessary, but the way she's looking at me, with another one of those bright smiles on her face, is enough to silence my doubts.

"So, what's the occasion then? What are we getting all spruced up for?" Jason asks.

I clear my throat. "Family reunion."

He pauses what he's doing for a moment and makes eye contact via the mirror. "Difficult family?"

I nod. Violet squeezes my hand and smiles at me again.

"Ugh, I'm sorry. I know all about what *that's* like. But not to worry, I'll have you looking your best in no time!" Jase carries on massaging shampoo into my scalp, and I close my eyes again.

Between his massage, and Violet caressing her fingers past mine, and the two of them chattering on every so often, I'm starting to feel my anxiety fade a little. I guess I'm starting to understand why girls like going to hairdressers so much. I didn't fully realize how much tension I'd been carrying, until some of it started melting away.

CHAPTER SIX

The transformation is subtle at first, but I can tell immediately. Chris looked so stressed ever since we got off the train. But now... His face is starting to relax, and the longer I carry on holding his hand, the more feedback he's giving me. At first, he was just clinging onto the armrest of the chair, but now... As I carry on teasing his fingers with mine, he's reciprocating, more so than before.

Now we're talking. He's getting more comfortable touching me, which is obviously great. At this rate, we'll be flirting up a storm by the time we get to my Airbnb. I can't wait. And yet...

Am I doing the right thing here? What am I risking in the process?

I try not to think about it right now. Our mission is clear; I already committed to the plan. And maybe this is exactly what I need right now. I'm helping him, sure, but that doesn't mean I can't get something out of the arrangement myself. I'm even enjoying just holding a guy's hand again. The uncertainty of where it might lead is the majority of the charm.

So, I keep quiet and just watch as Jase works his magic. Shampoo, moisturizing hair mask and a trim of Chris' hair, and a similar treatment for the beard.

"You've got some amazing growth," Jase remarks, while running his fingers through Chris' beard. "How long did it take?"

He mumbles something about a few months, which seems to impress Jase. All I can think about is how it would feel to run*my* fingers through there. God, I love a man with a nice beard. And thick, unruly hair. Except for the few extra pounds he carries, Chris is pretty much exactly my usual type. He's not a bad boy, though, which is definitely a good thing. Bad boys are trouble, 100% of the time. I've already learned that the hard way with Sam. To think that I actually thought that asshole was the one. Ugh.

The longer I watch them, the more in awe I am. I was trying to make a point back on the train when I argued with Chris about him being my type. But actually... I wasn't lying at all. With just a few little tweaks...

By the time Jase blow-dries his hair and styles his beard with a little bit of product, my heart is starting to race. I can barely look away now. God, and those deep blue eyes are just the icing on this great big beefcake.

"Awesome job, Jase," I mumble. "Wow!"

He grins at me, then at Chris in the mirror. "All done!"

"We're going to need some more of that stuff for tomorrow." I point at the little tub he used to set Chris' beard.

"Sure thing." Jase gets up, picks up a fresh one off the glass shelf on the wall, and pops it into a little bag before handing it to me with a wink. "Anything else I can help you lovebirds with?"

I smile and glance shyly at Chris, who is leaning forward and checking himself out in the mirror. "Nope, that's it."

I hand Jase my credit card.

"Whoa, wait a minute, I should get that!" Chris complains behind me.

"It's already done." Jase quickly scans it and hands it back to me with a grin. "Have a nice night, you two!"

"Oh, we will," I say. "See you later!"

We grab our bags, which had been waiting just by the door, and leave the shop. Only then do I realize just how flustered I am by the whole experience. Suddenly I no longer know what to say or do.

But as soon as Chris joins my side, and I'm able to slip my hand into the crook of his arm, I start to feel better. Safer.

"Where to now?" he asks.

I had planned to do some shopping tonight. Not

just for him, but for myself as well. Mostly, I was planning a stroll down memory lane through the little boutiques I used to frequent when I studied here. But my interest in that has suddenly waned...

"I think this has done the job nicely. We should get that pizza and turn in for the evening."

He sighs loudly. "Thank god; I'm starving."

So am I. Just not necessarily for pizza. Within the span of about forty minutes with Jase, Chris has turned from teddy bear cute into total fucking hotness. And he's coming home with me! I'm not that kind of girl and yet, right now, I kind of am.

Every time I catch him glancing over at me, it warms me in new and exciting places. For the first time in many months, I'm ready to do *that* again with a guy. Not to do him a favor, but purely for me. Who even am I anymore? Is this what guys feel like when they're out on the prowl? It's addictive.

"Just around the corner," I mumble under my breath. A shiver creeps down my spine as we reach the edge of the Old Town. Am I about to get everything I've been fantasizing about? What will he be like once we're all alone together?

But first, dinner. When we enter the pizza joint which is set back from the crowded main street in another little alley, tempting aromas of roasted cheese and pepperoni surround us. I can't enjoy it like I usually do. I'm too preoccupied, too distracted by

Chris' presence.

"Hiya, what can I get you?" The girl at the register sounds as bored as ever, while chewing lazily on a piece of gum. If it wasn't for the great pizza, her attitude would have put me off years ago when I still lived here. I'm shocked she hasn't been fired.

I turn to Chris. "I usually used to get the Quattro Stagioni, but everything's great here. What do you feel like?"

His eyes meet mine, and my stomach seems to drop immediately. Good lord. I don't know how I'm coherent right now.

"Quattro Stagioni is good with me."

"Cool. A large one. To take away," I tell the girl, who has been impatiently tapping her gel nails against the counter throughout. Impatient cow. And still, her incessant chewing is getting on my nerves even more.

"That's all?" she asks, while staring at Chris, especially. It's super awkward, the way she's looking him up and down. More so because he instantly notices and looks uncomfortable.

Even so, her question makes me think. One pizza isn't going to be enough, is it? A guy as huge as him must have quite the appetite, especially after spending nearly half a day on a train. And I'm making things even weirder by assuming otherwise.

"Do you want any sides? Chicken wings?" I ask him. "Or whatever else?"

He looks flustered, which makes me feel worse still. He seems to have some hangups about food, maybe that's why he wouldn't tell me his favorite dish back on the train. I decide to just add whatever sides I like. All of them. As if it's the most normal thing in the world.

"Okay, so we'll do a dozen hot wings, and some garlic knots, and two signature milkshakes, and... and Jalapeno poppers as well," I mumble. "And *that* will be all."

The girl rings up our order and disappears in the back shortly after.

"You'd better let me get this now," Chris says, while fishing his wallet out of his back pocket. His face is flushed, and I can feel the anxiety radiating off him.

"The food's worth it, I promise." I don't know if I'm saying it to reassure him or myself.

"How far to where you're staying?"

"Barely two minutes away."

He sighs and looks around. At anything, except me. Shit. We were doing so well earlier on the train. And now it's painfully weird all over again. I slip my hand into his, just to see his reaction. He doesn't really hold on to it like he did earlier.

"If you're having second thoughts about this, you know, I can just head home..." Chris tells me.

"Absolutely no second thoughts from my side.

Plus, I'm going to need help carrying all this stuff," I say.

"Right."

CHAPTER SEVEN

*** Chris ***

The wait at the pizza shop is excruciating. Mostly because Violet looks so uncomfortable throughout. She tries to hold my hand, but it feels forced now. I mean, it probably was forced all along. And now that we're about to be totally alone together, I guess it's getting a bit too real for comfort.

This was all pretend, after all. She must be concerned about having me—a total stranger—in her room all night. I wish I knew how to tell her she has nothing to worry about. I just hope there's a couch. Or else I'll just take the floor. I've certainly slept in worse conditions.

Jesus, I should have never agreed to any of this.

"Chris," she whispers.

This is it. This is when she tells me she's changed her mind.

"Yep?" I glance at her from the corner of my eye and brace, not sure for what.

"Favorite movie?"

I shake my head. What's the point of playing this

game anymore? When it's so obvious that this stupid, impulsive plan of hers is about to fall to pieces.

"Or TV series. I've been planning on re-watching *Stranger Things* all the way from the beginning to prepare for the new season."

"I love *Stranger Things*," I tell her, almost on autopilot.

"Cool. We can watch it together, then." She smiles briefly, squeezes my hand, and runs her thumb across my knuckles. It feels so good, I close my eyes and try to breathe again. I don't know how I can still fall into this trap, when it's so obvious that that's all it is.

I don't know how long we stand there like that. Hand in hand. Trying and failing to catch a good breath. Until finally the girl returns from the kitchen with our order, all packed up in takeaway boxes. She stacks it all up high and places it on the counter while giving me one of those looks. The type I'm all too familiar with. A look full of disapproval and judgment. Because she knows how wrong this situation is. I don't belong here with Violet.

I don't belong anywhere.

I let go of Violet's hand and tap my credit card against the machine on the counter. Once the payment is done, I pick up the pile of boxes.

It's a lot. Way more than what Violet would have ordered normally, that's why she hesitated earlier. And still less than an average Tuesday night for me. I ought to be ashamed of myself.

Worse still, she's going to watch me eat. Shit.

I wish the earth would open up and swallow me now. Because I can bear a lot. I can look intimidating, so people tend to stare. It's okay, nothing new. But the prospect of outstaying my welcome with Violet... It's too much to bear.

A disgraceful slob, you are! Mother's voice reminds me. *Lazy and good for nothing like your father.* Who is now dead. Fuck.

"Ok, bye," Violet grumbles, while heading for the door, opening it so I can follow behind her with the food.

"I'm sorry about her fucking attitude," Violet complains. "She's even grumpier than I remember."

"It's okay."

"Really, I mean it. I hope you didn't tip her."

I keep quiet, because of course I did. We walk in silence until we stop at a door which is indeed just a minute's walk away. Just as well, because I'm beat.

" *You're* not having second thoughts now, are you?" she asks.

"*Me?*" I blurt out.

"It's just... I mean you're barely looking at me. Like you have something to say but don't know how to say it."

"I guess... I just want to tell you not to worry about it if you want me to go. You've already done more for me than necessary."

"Actually..." She makes a face and shrugs. And I brace for rejection.

"Yeah?"

"You're doing me a favor by coming back here." She turns away and rests her arm on the door before looking back at me with sad eyes.

"I don't get it."

"I... It's been so nice talking to you on the train, and—last time I was here was with… well, you get the idea. I never told you on the train, because it didn't seem right, but I'm meant to be attending an engagement party tomorrow night, of all things, and..." She shrugs and forces a sad smile, which gets my heart racing again.

That's what was missing. She hasn't smiled at me in a while. And as a result, I felt like I outstayed my welcome. Maybe her change in attitude wasn't about me at all; she's been wrapped up in her own thoughts and memories.

"I guess I really didn't want to be alone tonight, if that makes sense," she adds.

"Makes sense."

"Thanks, Chris." With those two simple words, she perks up a little. And I experience another new feeling. The feeling of being needed. Shit, I would do anything she asks, as long as she rewards me with another smile.

She checks her phone and types in the security code to unlock the door and pushes it open. I enter right behind her, making sure I don't bang the corners of the pizza box into the door frame or anything else. It's a challenge. It's an even bigger challenge to get past Violet, allowing her to close and lock the door behind us.

"Up the stairs and straight through," she tells me.

I follow her directions and put the food down, while catching my breath. Only then do I look around a bit. The Airbnb is unusual. It's just a loft, with a couch and coffee table, bed and basic kitchenette all in one spacious room. The pitched roof and wooden beams overhead give the space a chapel-like effect.

The wall at the far end features a huge monochrome mural which reminds me of M.C. Escher's mind-bending prints, except lighter and more cheerful. I can't look away from it. Violet told me she paints murals professionally. This can't be a coincidence, surely?

"One of yours?" I point at the wall.

She nods. "One of my first paid commissions. The owner of this place is so happy with it, he gives me a special deal whenever I'm in town."

I'm in awe. "That's amazing. You're super talented."

"Thanks." She blushes and averts her gaze from me. It's adorable. *She's* adorable.

She kicks her shoes off and makes a beeline for what I assume to be the bathroom, leaving me alone for a couple of minutes. I'm still staring at the giant painting when she returns.

"Here. Your sweatshirt." She holds it up in my direction after plucking a couple of long blonde hairs off it. Honestly, I might have preferred it with the hair. To remind me that today actually happened and I didn't just imagine it all. I quickly turn to face her again.

"Ah, you're welcome to keep it if you want," I mumble. Just why she would want it, now that she can change into something else from her luggage, I'm not sure. What a stupid thing to say.

She hugs it against herself and smiles up at me. "It's a nice one, though. Tell you what. Whenever I want it, I'll just borrow it again."

"Any time." I stare at her. She stares up at me with those big puppy eyes of hers. Time seems to stand still.

And then, almost in slow motion, she puts the sweatshirt down on the sofa beside us and approaches me. My heart is racing so fast, I nearly forget how to breathe. She stretches her arms out at me, making me freeze like an absolute idiot.

"Thanks for taking such good care of me earlier. I surely would have frozen half to death if not for you," she says. Her hands rest on my shoulders, and I instinctively put mine on her waist.

God damn, this is even hotter than our first hug on the train. I barely know what to do with myself when she tightens her arms around my neck, forcing me to yield and bend down in her direction until our bodies touch completely.

My knees, already sore and tired after being stuck in that train seat for nearly five hours, threaten to buckle. I take a deep whiff of her hair and nearly lose my balance when her floral perfume hits my lungs.

Christ, how did I get here? How am I allowed to do this with her? This cannot be real. Her fingers caress the side of my face. Her endlessly gray eyes continue to stare into mine. And she's smiling again. I could kill for that smile.

"I want you to know that I don't normally do this," she whispers.

I shake my head. Same here. I don't *ever* do this.

"I haven't even really talked to a guy, since..." Her eyes well up again, but only briefly, before she blinks the moisture away. Since she got cheated on. I understand.

"It's okay," I say, but no sound is coming.

She gestures at the sofa with her eyes. I nearly stumble backwards trying to get to it. But there's no time to fixate on my clumsiness. As soon as I sit down, she kneels next to me and wraps her arms around my neck again.

"You're a great guy, Chris," she tells me.

I shake my head. No. No, I'm not.

"All the shit you're going through, and your first instinct was to take care of me instead," she says.

Isn't that just normal, though? Anybody would have done that in my place. And what about her? I told her about the funeral and her reaction was to offer to tag along. Who even does that? An angel, that's who.

But all I manage to say is: "Likewise." My voice sounds funny to my own ears. Weak and flat. And that phrase did nothing to express the depth of my gratitude.

She runs her fingers through my beard, which is... It's deadly. She smiles and closes her eyes for a moment, before looking at me again. "You know, I just adore a nice full beard on a guy. So handsome. Kills me without fail."

She's the one killing me, though. Her entire being. The hungry look in her eyes. The way she subtly licks her lips, probably without being aware she's doing it. The way her chest rises and falls with urgent breaths. I don't know what happened between the disaster at the pizza shop and our arrival here, but the change in her is like night and day. Suddenly I no longer feel like an intruder, but like she truly wants me here. And I don't even know what I did to deserve it.

"I..." I don't know what to say either. I barely

know up from down anymore.

"This would be a good time to compliment me back." She grins at me. *Argh.* The way she teases is deadly too.

"Jesus, Violet. Where would I even start?"

"Wherever you want. I'm your girlfriend, remember? And you're my boyfriend. Nothing's off limits." Those words make the hairs on the back of my neck stand up, they're so alien.

She continues to look me in the eye, and starts running her fingers through my hair. I couldn't break eye contact if I wanted to, that's how spellbound I am.

"That's what you want? Truly?"

She nods. "Truly."

"If you're my girlfriend, then..." I whisper. Oh my, the possibilities. I'm not sure I can allow myself to consider any of them. This is all just a game and I mustn't forget it.

"I *am* your girlfriend." She leans in with parted lips. I know what I want more than anything.

The peck on the lips in the train was magical, but it left me wanting. Aching. Dying for more. In a sudden bout of courage, or recklessness, I grab her pretty little face and guide it closer to me. She scoots ahead as close to me as possible. Her legs press up against my thigh; one of her hands rests on the side of my cheek, the other on my shoulder.

I feel her breaths quicken against my lips as she leans in closer and... She's the first to introduce a little tongue. She wraps her arm around my neck and merges into me, kissing, licking, tasting me. Somehow she ends up in my lap, sitting awkwardly across my thighs, pressed up into my stomach, making it impossible to ignore just how mismatched we are.

Me, the big clumsy ape I've always been, and her… Perfection wrapped up in a pretty little package. But as my cheeks and ears heat up with embarrassment, and I try to stop this mistake from getting any worse, she whimpers my name into my mouth, and clings to me as if her life depends on it.

I could scream. I could cry. I want to thank her for giving me this experience. For letting me do something which other people might take for granted. Something, which if not for her, I would have never known. At the same time, I want to stop her. To shake some sense into her and ask her what the fuck she thinks she's doing. She doesn't have to; she doesn't owe me anything. And if it's just company she wants tonight, she doesn't need to give me any piece of herself in return.

But I can't tell her any of this. I can only sit back helplessly as she straddles me, caresses my face, and plays with my hair, and kisses me like a guy like me doesn't deserve to be kissed. And she's oblivious to my silent protest, which continues to scream inside my own mind, but which I fail to express in any way.

Stop, Violet! Stop it! Stop touching me!

Her hand grabs one of mine, which has been white knuckling the armrest of the sofa, and puts it on the side of her hip. Good Lord, I'm unworthy.

Then she cups my face and kisses me so deeply, it's like she's giving me life.

Leave me alone, Violet! You don't have to do this! Don't touch me!

... Please, don't ever stop!

CHAPTER EIGHT

*** Violet ***

Our first proper kiss blows my mind. Never have I ever brought a guy back with me on a first date. Or without even going on a real date. Or for a one night stand. Or whatever this is.

Never have I ever felt this way during a first kiss or first make-out session.

Never have I ever wanted anyone this much.

But Chris isn't just anyone. He isn't a bad boy with an attitude. He isn't a player who could replace me in the blink of an eye. He's technically a stranger, and yet someone I already feel closer to than anyone I've ever dated.

He's *real*. He's a saint. A million times the man Sam could ever aspire to be.

He's also absolutely overcome. Sunk back into the sofa with his eyes tightly shut, he's trying desperately to catch his breath while keeping up with me. Kissing, teasing, downright devouring my tongue as if his life depends on it. My god, he's full of passion. I could have never guessed he had it in him. All he needed was for someone to pull the release.

It's an honor. A privilege. An absolute joy.

And I'm hotter than I've ever been. For a guy I might never have paid attention to had we not been sitting next to each other. Well, I lie. He might be a saint, but I'm not.

If I'd seen him anywhere else, I might have noticed the mess of blond hair and the beard, the broad shoulders, how fucking tall he is, as well as those gloriously blue eyes of his and thought: 'Hm, shame. He'd be so hot if only he'd lost a few pounds.'

And I would have been so wrong. Because that caveat is unnecessary. Chris is alreadyhot. Just as he is. Well, Jase's little tweaks certainly helped me see it fully, but even otherwise... Holy shit, Chris was drop dead gorgeous all along.

"Stop," he gasps.

Did I hear that right? I slow down to make sure.

He pushes my hand away, which had started to tug the hem of his shirt upwards. "Violet, stop!"

The urgency in his voice makes me flinch away. "What's wrong?"

He opens his eyes and looks at me, pleading: "Please, stop!"

"I'm sorry, I thought you were into it," I stammer. Did I misread the situation that badly just now? Fuck.

I try to slip off his lap, but find that his hand is still resting firmly on my hip and not letting me move away. That would be even hotter, if I wasn't so confused by the sudden mood swing.

"I... Jesus, how do I even say this without sounding like a complete loser?" he says.

"You can tell me anything," I whisper. "And I don't think you're a loser."

He pinches the bridge of his nose and shakes his head. "Violet, you don't know a damn thing about me. You cannot do this."

"Tell me, then," I stammer, still shocked at how quickly the vibe shifted. Am I that oblivious to other people's thoughts and feelings? Probably. That's why it was so easy for them to betray me. Maybe I had it coming.

"You've brought me—essentially a complete stranger—here, to... I don't know... For company? You didn't want to be alone, you said?" Chris says.

"Well, I suppose. Pathetic as that sounds," I say. *Who's the loser now, huh?*

He shakes his head. "Not pathetic, but... This doesn't have to be anything else. I'm perfectly fine with just that."

"You don't want to... Do. Anything. Else?" I ask. *Fuck.* He doesn't fancy me. So back on the train when I was questioning him about his type, and he said he doesn't have one and tried to flip things around on himself, he was just trying to be nice. To let *me* down easy.

My cheeks burn up bright red. "I'm so sorry. I didn't want to make you uncomfortable."

Ugh! I just wish he'd said something sooner. I thought the feeling was mutual! After all the cuddling on the train, the hand-holding, the eye contact, and the way he kept looking at my body every so often, as if he couldn't help it... Am I really that delusional? Or that desperate to feel something again?

"Oh no, you didn't! But I don't want you to do anything, that—" he stops mid-sentence.

I frown. "What?"

"I don't know! I don't know what's happening here anymore!" he exclaims. "We were supposed to *pretend* to be a couple. Tomorrow. In front of my family. And now we're here, and—"

His outburst confuses me even further. I close my eyes, take a deep breath, and slowly exhale through my mouth. That only marginally soothes my shame.

"We're talking past each other, I think," I conclude, in as steady a voice as I can manage. "Let's not do that. Let's just talk, like we were doing on the train earlier."

"Okay."

"Before you answer me, know I'm a big girl and I can take it. Whatever it is you want to say. Just please don't lie to me."

"Okay," he repeats.

"I know we discussed pretending a bunch of stuff.

And that's all fine. We'll still do that tomorrow, no matter how this conversation turns out. But right now, we're alone. We have no need to pretend."

"Right, that's what I've been trying to say!" he exclaims.

"When I asked you to stay, and said you'd be doing me a favor, I wasn't pretending then."

"Okay."

"Neither was I pretend-kissing you." I take another deep breath before asking my next question. "Were you?"

He stares at me for a moment. The look in his eyes is pure panic. "No."

His answer allows me to breathe again. That's a relief.

"Then, what's the problem?" I ask.

He averts his gaze and makes a face.

"Please. Just be honest with me. Like you've been honest with me about your family and stuff already," I whisper, while softly placing my hand on the side of his face. Holy shit, there's so much tension between us, that simple touch hits me like an electric shock.

He shakes his head. "You have to understand, I'm... I'm..."

"Just tell me. Please," I whisper.

"I don't fucking know how this works, okay? I don't know what I'm doing here! I don't know how to do whatever it is we're doing. I certainly don't fucking know what to do next! I—"

"Chris, sweetheart. I'm nervous too," I say, and start to caress his face. He leans into it with his eyes half-shut, which means everything to me. "Ever since we left Jase's, I've been shitting bricks, because I really fucking like you. And I didn't know if you like me back, or you're just going along with things because it's easier that way. And I didn't want you to think that whatever happens between us is just meaningless bullshit. And worse still, I don't know how I'm ever going to say goodbye to you after tomorrow..."

I look up at him, and he looks at me. My eyes are sticky, which makes it annoyingly hard to focus. And as long as he keeps quiet, I still don't fucking know where he stands. But I can't force an answer out of him either, because then he might just tell me whatever I want to hear. Fuck. This is why I could never do a one night stand. Because I can't keep my emotions in check and get too damn invested!

"You *like* me?" he asks.

"I *really* like you," I whisper. "What did you think? I just pick up random guys, cuddle with them on the train while wearing their clothes, give up my hair appointment for them, invite them to stay in my room… All the while, telling every single one of them that I don't normally do this, before making out with them on the couch the moment we walk in while my favorite takeaway pizza in the whole world is getting cold?"

"I don't know!" Chris says. I'd be annoyed at his response, if he didn't look so damn lost saying it.

"Well, I don't do *any* of that. Normally." I sigh, let go of his face, and lean back. There. I've said my piece. Now it's up to him. Break my heart. I'm ready.

"I..." He clears his throat. "Violet. I really like you too."

That's it, my brain just about explodes. I can't help but raise my voice in frustration. "Then what's the fucking problem?!"

"The problem is, I'm a virgin! That just now was my first real kiss. Back on the train was the first time I ever held a girl's hand. I don't know how any of this stuff works. *That's* the fucking problem!"

I throw my hands up in the air in frustration. "I know all that already!"

His face falls further, if that's even possible. "How?"

"You've dropped enough hints about it for me to connect the dots." I shrug. It wasn't exactly rocket science.

"And you're still..."

"I still really like you," I say. The way his eyes soften every time I tell him I like him means everything to me right now. "And I still want to kiss you. And I still want whatever it is you would want to do next. No pressure."

It occurs to me that throughout our conversation, his hand remained exactly where it was, firmly grasping my hip. It hasn't moved even a fraction of an inch. And that's fucking hot. Everything about him is. If I'm totally honest, the fact that I'm the first girl he's ever done anything intimate with is... Oh my God, it's the absolute hottest. And the way he was kissing me earlier... So frantic; almost desperate... If that's anything like how he will be should we take things further, that's enough to melt my panties all the way off.

"But... You could do so much better than me," he mumbles. Almost as if he's talking to himself and not me.

I shake my head. "No, I couldn't. I couldn't possibly find a nicer, more caring guy than you."

"Who cares about nice and caring? I'm a fucking mess, don't you get it? I've spent ten years trying to run from my past, and yet every night I close my eyes to try and sleep, I'm right back where I started. And tomorrow, I have to go back and I just know it's going to hit me like a freight train as soon as I walk through the door."

My heart is racing, as are my thoughts. I want to argue with him. I want to tell him that that was then, and this is now. And that things will be fine. That's exactly why I offered to go with him, so that he wouldn't have to face his past alone. That if he confronts his mom about all the shit she's done to him, and gets his family on his side, he will somehow emerge victorious and reborn.

Instead, I bite my lip so hard it's starting to hurt. Because all that is a whole lot of bullshit. Who the hell do I even think I am, that my presence by his side is going to make such a big difference? It's still going to be probably one of the most harrowing experiences of his life. It's still going to hurt and stir up old trauma. He's still going to suffer. Whether I'm there with him or not.

"Tomorrow is going to be one of the worst days of your life," I conclude.

When his eyes meet mine, they're wide with shock.

"Alrighty then, Miss Positivity," he stammers.

"I don't mean to be flippant. Tomorrow is going to suck on so many levels. You'll be forced to face all those things you've been trying to forget. And it's going to hurt. Deeply. And what's worse is, you'll have to deal with the realization that your dad is gone forever too."

Chris just stares at me now. His grip on me fades, his bottom lip trembles, and his breaths grow more and more unsteady.

"And that's why I offered to come along, before I even knew a damn thing about you. Because *nobody* should have to go through that alone."

I take a deep breath. "Least of all the good, kind-hearted man I'm in the process of falling head over heels for. Because when I said I really like you, that's what I *actually* meant."

"I don't know what to say..."

"You don't have to say anything," I say.

"I've never had anyone who was willing to—"

"Now you do. I don't know how much of a difference it will make, but I'll be there every step of the way. I'll be your backup. Your reinforcements. I'll try to catch you if you fall and I'll be your shoulder to cry on if you need it. Because when I really like someone, I try to give everything I can."

His lips quiver as he inhales deeply and just stares at me. The silence between us now is far from awkward, no matter how loaded it has become. Because there's that softness again in his eyes. That means he's starting to believe me.

"It'll make all the difference," he whispers, while reaching for my face.

I hope so. I melt into his arms, nuzzling, kissing the crook of his neck, enjoying the tickle of his beard against my forehead, while wrapping my arms around him as best I can. And there's that feeling of safety again bubbling up in my chest as I catch a deep whiff of his intoxicating scent. It's that sensation which tries to convince me that as long as he's by my side, I'll be invincible. I would have never told another guy all the stuff I just said to him. And I would have never invited anyone else home with me either. God, I love this feeling. So full of promise and hope. I haven't felt this high in a long time, probably ever.

"Where did you come from, Violet?"

I suppress a smile. "I was always around… I just wish we'd met sooner." Oh, how I wish we'd met before I got with Sam. How hopeful I was back then, before he shattered my heart into a million pieces. That's the version of me Chris deserved to see, not this… Jaded and full of self doubt.

"Me too…" He sighs deeply while continuing to caress my shoulders and back. It's distracting how good that feels. With every bit of his affection, another little crack in me starts to heal.

"You know…" I whisper.

"Mhmm?"

"Unless you're in a rush to get rid of me tomorrow—"

"Never!" His answer came so quickly, it made me smile all over again.

"We've got all the time in the world. We can just take it slow," I say.

He tightens his arms around me and sighs again. "I think… I'd like that."

I close my eyes and enjoy the feeling of being completely and utterly overwhelmed by his embrace. It's beautiful and serene, until my stomach lets out an embarrassingly loud growl.

"Heh, sorry. Maybe we should eat before the pizza gets completely cold, huh?" I chuckle.

He suppresses a smile and lets go of me with one hand, allowing me to swing my leg across him to sit sideways in his lap. He leans forward just enough to pull the takeaway boxes closer to us. All the while, I'm still draped across his thick, strong thighs, and in zero mood to get up. Luckily, he doesn't seem to expect me to.

He hands me one of the boxes, then another, which I balance on my thighs, as a makeshift table.

"What do you want to start with?" I ask.

He shrugs in silence. Oh yeah, he's weird about food. Maybe he'll relax if I don't make a big deal about it. I go straight for the biggest box containing the pizza and open it on my lap, handing one slice to him and picking up another for myself.

It's just as good as I remember, even though it's only lukewarm. Damn. There's no way I can contain my enjoyment, almost moaning as I chew and swallow that first bite. When I open my eyes after, I catch Chris grinning at me. He's actually adorable when he smiles. He doesn't do it nearly often enough.

"What? Told you it was my favorite!" I say, before taking another bite, and savoring it with my eyes shut.

CHAPTER NINE

*** Chris ***

Just how Violet managed to make eating a slice of pizza seductive and funny all at the same time, I'll never know. But it does break the tension between us. And her excitement is infectious, because this is by far the best pizza I've ever had. I've eaten a lot of pizza over the years, so that's saying something.

Probably, it's mostly her company. I've never had a better person to share a meal with. And she's still sitting in my lap, like it's the most normal thing in the world.

So many firsts.

A part of me is disappointed that I blurted out everything I just did, and stopped where we were heading. But I had to. The closer Violet got to taking my t-shirt off, the more I panicked. It's not her fault. She couldn't know. If I have my way, she'll never find out.

Every so often she smiles at me in between bites of food, and I'm in awe again. Can't stop admiring her—no, worshiping her with my eyes, while following her example.

Before long, the pizza, as well as most of the ridiculous combination of sides she ordered, is finished. I couldn't keep track of how much I ate. That tends to happen to me a lot. That's my biggest problem.

But she didn't notice any of that. At least the way she's looking at me hasn't changed. I'm still welcome. I'm still wanted.

And when we discard the empty boxes on the table, and focus on each other again, I still recognize that same hunger in her eyes which stumped me earlier. Because I still can't believe it's for me.

But we're going to take it slow. Slow is good. Slow is safe. Slow doesn't require me to expose anything I don't want to.

Still, it takes about two minutes of loaded glances and gentle kisses to end up right where we started. With our lips and hands seeking each other out.

This time, I'm ready for it. Sort of.

This time, I don't freak out and tell her to stop, when all I really need is for her to carry on.

This time, when I get hard because she's straddling my thighs, I try to enjoy it. I refuse to make the same mistake again.

This time, I love everything she gives me. Because I realize how precious it is. How rare.

Hell, I already knew how rare it was, that's why I

couldn't believe it was meant for me. Her affections are too pure. Too good to be true. Certainly too good for me. But here we are. Sharing a moment of perfection.

She said earlier that she's falling for me. No way that's true, even if she believes it to be. Still, just for tonight, I'll try to believe it too. I'll try to savor it. Because I've already fallen for her. I'm already lost, if not for her arms around my shoulders, and her lips on mine. Come tomorrow, reality will set in, and all the magic we're sharing now will be gone. She'll see who I really am and where I came from, and change her mind about me.

But for this brief moment, all seems right in the world. On the sofa, making out until our lips are sore, and later on in the bedroom, cuddling and caressing each other until she falls asleep.

***

It's the morning of the worst day of my life, probably. Ever since Violet referred to it as that last night, I tried not to worry about it too much and just focus on her. If my willpower alone could make time stand still, we would still be in bed, kissing and cuddling like we did for hours on end before she dozed off, and I couldn't stop admiring her then too.

Even just waking up with her head resting against my shoulder was magic like I've never experienced before. But now, all that is over. All the peace I felt, cocooned into the duvet beside her, has faded. Instead, it's been replaced with a mixture of terror and resignation.

We've reached my childhood home, the one place in the world I vowed I would never return, just in time to face the firing squad. The door is open, and there's a small gathering of familiar faces collected inside. Fuck, it even smells the same. Stale cigarettes and despair.

"You made it, then?" That's the voice that has been haunting my nightmares.

Violet squeezes my hand, and I feel my back straighten just a little bit as I glance at Mother. She's sitting in that same old armchair. In the same old living room. Everything is exactly as I remember it. Nothing has changed, except... Everything is a little older, a little shabbier, and a little smaller than I remember, too.

I glance over at Dad's side of the sofa. Uncle Fred is sitting there instead now. He has aged as much as the surroundings. Off to the side of the sofa are the twins, my cousins. When I left, they were about seven, but they're practically grown now. And Aunt Helen, who barely looks up at me while having a hushed conversation with the next door neighbor.

Uncle Fred gets up and shakes my hand.

"Sorry for your loss, son," he tells me.

I nod. What else can I do?

"This is Violet, my girlfriend," I mumble awkwardly, at no one in particular. It's still weird to say that word, even though we practiced a few times on the bus over here.

"Uncle Fred," I tell her under my breath as they silently shake hands. "Mom's brother."

Mother, meanwhile, is flat-out glaring at the two of us. She isn't even trying to hide her hostility in front of the rest of the people present. It puts me on a back foot, because it makes me wonder if she ever hid her true colors at all. And if she didn't, that means...

That means that they knew. It means they approved of her behavior. Because nobody ever did a damn thing to intervene.

"We should probably leave for the funeral home soon," Uncle Fred says. "Are you both riding with us?"

I shrug. "If there's room in the car, sure."

"So this is how you greet me, a grieving widow, after ten years away," Mother complains.

Always playing the victim card. While still being the worst person in the room.

"I'm not here for you. I'm here for Dad," I say.

"See, Fred? I knew he would do something like this. What I never expected is that he would humiliate the family by bringing some floozy with him. That's wholly inappropriate."

I'm tensing up, almost shaking. "Violet is my *girlfriend*." I enunciate the word more clearly this time. Her thumb brushes past my knuckles, which only barely manages to calm me down. Glimpses of her pretty eyes staring at me throughout last night's marathon make-out session fill my mind, just long enough to ground me. "She's *my* family." *More than any of you lot, even though I've only just met her.*

Mother scoffs loudly, which sparks a coughing fit. I guess she's still on two packs a day, minimum. And still she managed to outlive Dad. The universe is unfair.

Uncle Fred shakes his head. "I wish you'd both leave those old arguments in the past where they belong. Just for one day."

The fact that he's referencing me along with her is pissing me off even further. I knew I wouldn't find any allies here. Literally no one. Except Violet. Who volunteered to step into this cesspit all on her own. She must be regretting that decision already.

I glance over at her and find her already looking up at me. For a moment, I threaten to drown in the depths of her gray eyes. "You'll be okay," she mouths. Those lips have magical powers. And they taste pretty sweet as well.

While I don't fully believe her, I sure am glad she's here.

Uncle Fred walks past both of us. My two cousins,

who so far have barely looked up from their phones, follow closely behind. Aunt Helen shakes her head at me in that cool, nonchalant manner of hers, before helping Mother up out of her chair and ushering her out of the room.

All the while, I'm trying to breathe, and not to get overwhelmed in the flood of bad memories this place sparks. So many fights. So many beatings, and worse. Violet remains right by my side, holding my hand and resting her other hand on my upper arm.

"See what I mean now? Maybe it was a mistake for me to come back at all," I say.

She squeezes my hand. "I don't think so. I think if you'd skipped his funeral, you would have regretted it later."

Maybe. Or maybe this all will lead me to seek out the nearest bottle to crawl into. Dad's old hiding places probably wouldn't have changed while I've been gone. And while I drown my memories of this place, Violet will see a glimpse of the real me and run. As she should.

"Are you coming?" Uncle Fred's voice startles me out of my doomsday spiral.

"Yeah. Sorry."

"I'm super proud of you," Violet tells me, while we walk out of the house, towards Uncle Fred's old dark blue station wagon. Yet another thing that's still the same, except for the rust spots bubbling through the fenders.

While we're getting in, Aunt Helen's car pulls away already. In it there's Mother, and a couple of ladies I recognize from the neighborhood. I'm glad we're in separate cars. The more distance we keep throughout this experience, the better.

It's a bit of a struggle fitting my long legs in, even after pushing the seat all the way back. Once I'm settled, I'm still so tightly packed in I can't even turn to check on Violet, who took the space behind me. But when I feel her hand on my shoulder, I relax a little. It's crazy how she manages to put me at ease. We haven't even known each other for 24 hours, and yet her presence alone allows me to breathe.

"Your dad missed you a lot, towards the end," Uncle Fred says.

"Mhm."

"Your mum too. As did we, these last ten years," he continues.

"Oh, I highly doubt that she did." Or maybe she just missed having another target for her vitriol.

"I'll never understand the rift between you guys. She would never tell me what happened."

I scoff. And then I immediately regret it, because of how much that makes me sound like her. "I bet she didn't."

"Well, nevermind," Uncle Fred says. "For the service, did you want to say a few words?"

His question shocks me. "I wouldn't know what to say; I haven't prepared anything."

Violet's hand squeezes my shoulder, and I grab it and close my eyes. It's funny how such a simple gesture can affect me so deeply. Of course she said she'd be here with me, but the fact that she followed through… That means everything.

"Tomorrow, I'll be picking up the ashes," Uncle Fred says. "Your mum said she didn't want them, but I figured she might change her mind."

My throat tightens, and my eyes sting. I stare out of the window, at the familiar rows of brick houses passing me by. She hated him while he was still alive, and now that he's dead, she's happy to literally discard him, like the ratty old mattress and broken washing machine lying in one of the front yards along the way. Typical.

"I should have come home sooner," I whisper, as the first tear trickles down the side of my face and into my beard. I wipe it away with the back of my hand before turning to Uncle Fred. "I think I might want his ashes, if that's okay."

"Sure, son. Whatever you want."

CHAPTER TEN

*** Violet ***

The cremation was a simple affair, and the only people in attendance were those who were already at the house when we first arrived. Nobody said anything in remembrance, and there weren't any flowers or anything fancy for the wake either. It was even more depressing than I ever could have predicted. Chris held up remarkably well, though, possibly because he and his mom stayed as far away from each other as possible throughout.

And nobody spoke a word.

Now we're back at the house, which smells of dust and cigarette smoke. There's a buffet of dry looking sandwiches and watered down coffee. Chris doesn't touch any of it, and neither do I. The air is heavy with unspoken tension. Even if Chris hadn't told me anything, it would have been obvious all the same. All my instincts are telling me to run. I can only imagine how he must feel.

We're standing off to the side, my hand resting on his arm again, which is probably more to steady my own nerves than his at this point. His mom is silently glaring at us from the sofa all the way on the other side of the drawing room, in between bites of sawdust sandwich and sips of shitty coffee.

What shocked me most so far wasn't her. I knew she'd be a piece of work. It was his uncle, Fred. How nice and genuine he appeared to be. Is it all a farce? Was he a part of everything that happened, or just willfully ignorant?

Is it really possible that he didn't know anything? I find that hard to believe. There would have been signs. At the very least, cuts and bruises.

I want to ask Chris, but there isn't any chance to. And looking at him, I can see how on edge he is. How close to breaking. It makes me nervous, because I don't know him well enough to predict what would happen if he does. Will I be able to make good on my promises from last night? Of course I'd never leave him alone. But will I even be any help at all?

Can anyone be? Only he knows what he's going through.

His breaths are shallow. Fast. He's so tense. I can feel it through his sleeve, and even just hanging in the air around him. And so, I'm tense too. Bracing myself for I don't know what.

Plus, he's been drinking. Subtly, while sneaking into another room every so often. Thinking nobody would notice, probably, but I can smell it on him. I don't blame him, of course. And it doesn't change my resolve of standing by his side through all this. But it concerns me nonetheless, because I don't know how it'll affect him.

"...abandoned me. Ungrateful as usual—" his mother's voice pierces the murmur of conversation all around.

Chris takes a step forward, almost shaking me off. "Ungrateful for *what?*"

Oh shit, here we go.

"Ungrateful for the life I gave you! You nearly killed me when you were born, don't you know? You were so big even then, you nearly tore me in half!"

"Of course everyone knows that, because you don't miss the chance to complain about it. Well, I didn't ask to be born in the first place. You have only yourself to blame for that!"

"See?" She looks around the room. "See how he talks to me?"

"Won't you two just bury the hatchet already!" Uncle Fred interjects.

"Never," both say in unison.

"Over my dead body," his mom snaps.

"Not a moment too soon," Chris adds. "Should have been you in that casket today. Not him."

His aunt, who has been sitting next to his mom, sighs and shakes her head disapprovingly. And the twin teenage girls who I gather are her and Uncle

Fred's kids tentatively look up from their phones to see what's going on. Within seconds, they're furiously tapping away again, no doubt updating their friends of the unfolding drama.

"Chris, son. Why? Why so angry?" his uncle asks, almost dejectedly.

Chris turns, his eyes shooting daggers at everyone in the room. I barely recognize him; that's how enraged he looks. It's unnerving. Like Dr. Jekyll and Mr. Hyde.

"Ah, so many reasons. Too many to count, probably," he says.

His mother scoffs and shakes her head. "Always the drama queen. He's never had any sense. Makes everything about himself and spares no thought for what anyone else is going through."

"Look who's talking! Always playing the martyr around family and friends. But I know better. I know the real you. And so did Dad."

"Don't you talk about your father! You didn't give two shits about him or me when he was still around, and now you come in here—"

"*You* didn't give a shit about *him*. *You* probably killed him in the end!" Chris' outburst elicits a gasp from everyone in the room.

My throat closes up and my heart starts to race even faster. I try to steady myself with a deep breath, but I don't recall ever feeling this level of anxiety. It feels like life or death, but I can't decide who's in more danger yet.

"Now, son, that's completely uncalled for—" His uncle takes a couple of steps in Chris' direction.

Should I intervene before things escalate further? I suppose that's what I'm here for. I position myself in between the two large men and squeeze Chris' arm. He jerks away from me, but I don't give up and grab his arm again. The look he gives me is cold. Alien. Terrifying, if not for the shot of adrenaline coursing through my body.

"Say what you need to say," I tell him. "I'm with you."

He takes a breath, and I see a glimmer of the real him again. The sweet soul I met yesterday on the train. He doesn't try to retreat from me anymore. He straightens himself, and a new sense of calm seems to come over him, which allows me to catch a breath too.

"You all want reasons so badly? See if you can count them all yourself!" He looks down at himself for a split second, then starts unbuttoning his shirt.

A loud murmur passes through the room. The two teenage girls raise their phones, while talking in hushed voices. Are they literally recording this shit? Uncle Fred, who is still standing a couple of steps away from us, just looks helpless now.

And Chris' mother absolutely loses her mind,

shouting and cursing hysterically. "What the fuck are you doing? Behave yourself! They never should have given you the news! You should have stayed away like you do best!"

"Here are some reasons!" Chris is halfway done with his shirt. His fingers are trembling more and more now. He loses his patience and rips the rest of it open and throws it on the floor beside us. I'm taken aback myself. He turns, and our gazes meet only briefly, but long enough for me to see the tears glistening in his eyes.

"Here are some pretty big reasons at the back as well. Take a good look, everyone!" he shouts when he turns around.

Most of the people in the room were already stunned. Except his mother, who is still shrieking abuses, mostly about how disgusting and ugly he is, and how he should be ashamed of himself and cover up.

I just stand there, as if I'm no longer in control of my own body. When he stopped our make-out session halfway through last night, I thought he was just nervous because it was his first time. Maybe he was freaking out because our clothes were about to come off? Maybe he was trying to hide all this from me?

His torso is covered in scars. Their redness stands out sharply against his otherwise pale skin. Little round ones like the one I spotted under his sleeve yesterday–cigarette burns, I suppose. Longer ones on his back, maybe from a belt? I don't have the knowledge to be able to identify them. Is he ashamed of them? Maybe he just didn't want to have to explain.

Considering how his mom is reacting now, she probably tried to shame him into keeping himself covered at all times. Destroyed his confidence, simply so her dirty secret wouldn't be found out.

"And—" he turns again. "Some of them go back pretty far. I don't even remember when the first ones happened. But the rest… I can still feel them burn every day."

Tears are streaming down my face. I had no idea how bad things were. And I advised him to confront her? Shit, how stupid of me. Is he doing all this because I told him to? I'm not sure I could, in his stead. I wouldn't have survived what happened to him in the first place, probably. I'm not that strong. Or brave.

My heart is shattered. I don't know what to do, so I just stand there, shaking.

"There's your reasons. Feel free to ask my mother dearest for further clarifications. I'm fucking done with this fucking charade." He's visibly trembling too when he storms out of the room, right past me. And I'm still petrified.

"This was hardly the time or the place," I hear his aunt complain.

That snaps me out of my trance. "You ought to be ashamed of yourself! For caring more about his timing than the torture he had to face in this house as a child! Where the fuck were you when it was all happening? Where were any of you?" I scream.

Chris' mother glares at me. "You have no right to talk; you're not even a part of this family! You don't know what a menace he was, from the moment he learned how to crawl. He deserved everything that happened to him! My only regret is I didn't start disciplining him soon enough, or I might have been able to straighten him out!" She looks around for support, but everyone is awkwardly avoiding her gaze, so she trains her eyes on me again.

I glare right back. "He was just a little boy! A child! And you deserve to rot in prison!"

The two cousins stare at me with open mouths, until one of them giggles awkwardly. Shit. What am I still doing here? I gotta go find Chris.

I rush out of the room, past Uncle Fred, who seems to have turned to stone, and leg it out the door where I saw Chris go earlier. From there, through the dimly lit hallway and up the creaky carpeted stairs, I follow my instinct on where to go. I also follow the sound of doors slamming, and rummaging, until I arrive in what must have been his old bedroom. Once upon a time.

The room is filled with dusty boxes, which he is dragging around, emptying, and discarding one by one. The only reminder of its old purpose once upon a time is the single bed in the corner, and a torn Transformers poster on the wall.

I approach him and rest my hand on his bare shoulder. He jerks away.

"Don't fucking touch me!" he threatens.

"Chris," I plead. "Stop. Let me help you. What are you looking for?"

He pauses and closes his eyes while trying to catch his breath. "Just leave. Please just leave me alone." His voice is flat, monotone.

"I'll do whatever you want," I tell him. "Whatever you need. But not that. I'm not leaving you alone right now."

He sinks down into his knees, shivering, and I lean over him and place my hand on his shoulder again. He leans against the bed, still panting, before looking up at me in silence. Slowly, the tension in his back thaws a little, allowing him to take his first deeper breath.

"I'm so sorry—"

I shake my head. He has nothing to be sorry for.

"I humiliated you in front of everyone."

Huh? "What? No!"

"You were so sweet, offering to accompany me

today. And I—"

He suddenly leans forward and reaches for something under the bed. A dusty bottle of who knows what. His hands are shaking so hard, he's struggling to open it. So I take it from him, and without thinking, unscrew the cap before handing it back.

He takes a big swig, closes his eyes, and rests his head against the mattress behind him.

"I think you should go. Because I'm going to go ahead and finish this. And things are bound to get messy after that."

" *More* messy?" I blurt out.

He opens his eyes. "Please. Go. You don't need to see this. You didn't need to see any of this," he says, gesturing at himself.

"Sweetheart, I do need to. I promised I'd be here for you, and I'm not about to break that promise."

He shakes his head. "No. You're all kinds of lovely and I'm just no good—"

"Chris, Chris, Chris…" I shake my head and try to kneel next to him to get to his level, but there's so much crap and clutter lying everywhere, I have no room and end up sitting sort of on his thigh. I wrap my arms around his shoulders as best I can, while he turns his head away to take another sip. "Look at me, Chris."

"Mhm?"

"I'm so, so proud of you, Chris."

He shakes his head. "No, there's nothing to be proud of. I humiliated you."

"Babe, you humiliated your mother, not me. And rightly so." I watch him drink more. Jesus, how quickly is he going through that stuff? "Are you going to share, or…?"

He lowers the bottle. "I'm so sorry, Violet. I don't know how else to make it stop!"

I take the bottle and sniff its contents. "What is it, anyway?"

"I don't know. It's so long ago… I always kept something under the bed. Whatever I could get my hands on."

My heart breaks further. I take a small sip myself, closing my eyes as the sharp liquid burns its way down my throat. He used to drink this as a teenager. The only way he knew to cope, probably because that's what he'd seen others do. Did his dad drink too? It doesn't feel right to ask, so I keep my suspicions to myself.

Our eyes meet for a second. I guess it shows how much I hated the taste, because his expression twists in shame as he averts his gaze from me. "I still don't know how else—"

I put the bottle down and wrap my arms around him as tightly as I can, while somehow getting my other leg up and over his other thigh so I'm now straddling him on the floor. His arms steady me, reluctantly at first. But then, when I start caressing his hair, he sighs and rests his head against my chest, allowing me to tighten my arms around him.

"You don't make it stop. You let it happen," I whisper. "You sit and you feel it, and if you're up for it, you can tell me about all of it. Then, in time, it'll start to fade a little..."

His shoulders shudder deeply with every breath. I keep running my fingers through his hair as best I can, without loosening my embrace. He needs this. Shit, *I* need it too.

"You'll be okay. Maybe not today. Or tomorrow. But eventually..." I whisper, while kissing his hair again and again.

"I'm so proud I could stand with you while you did that. You confronted her. You told the truth..." I continue to cling to him, just as he falls apart completely. Breath by breath, I can feel him break in my arms.

"Why..." he cries.

I close my eyes, and just carry on holding him. This is what I'm here for. This is what I need to do. Give him space to express everything he's been bottling up all these years without interference or judgment.

"Why does she hate me so much?" he asks. "What did I ever do?"

I can't hold back the tears any longer either. Because that question has been on my mind too. And I just can't make sense of it. Why would a mother do this? It goes against every instinct. Against nature itself. The woman must be a sociopath.

"Babe, you didn't do anything. This isn't your fault," I whisper. "It was never your fault, you were just a kid."

A door creaks behind me, but Chris seems unaware. Until someone clears their throat and his whole body tenses up again, as if he's readying himself for a fight.

"Son…" It's Uncle Fred.

"Before you say anything, I'm not fucking apologizing!" Chris says.

I look up and watch as his uncle pushes aside some of the clutter on the bed and sits down, shaking his head continuously.

"I had no idea, son."

"No? You really didn't know?" I ask, remembering my earlier doubts. How the hell is that even possible?

"I'm so sorry…" Uncle Fred runs his hands through his hair. "In hindsight…"

Neither Chris nor I say anything. He hides in my arms again, so I carry on caressing his hair, until the tension in his shoulders melts once more.

"I suppose I should have seen the signs…"

Yeah, no shit, Sherlock!

"I thought you were just shy, and preferred to keep to yourself… I never questioned…"

Glancing at him from the corner of my eye, I spot the onset of tears.

I've never seen a grown man cry before today, and here's two of them in the same room together.

CHAPTER ELEVEN

* Chris *

Where am I? How did I get here?

I'm in my old room, and there's trash scattered everywhere on the floor. My old bed is digging painfully into my back, and my knees are weirdly folded and sore, weighed down by Violet.

Sweet Violet…

I take a deep breath and am surrounded by her, inside as well as out. With her scent filling my lungs, and her arms cradling my head against her soft sweater.

Or is it me who's gripping her first? Either way, I don't want to move a muscle, no matter how stiff my legs get.

"I'm so sorry," Uncle Fred's voice speaks behind me.

Oh yeah, he's here as well. For a split second, I readied myself to jump up and throw him out. I don't need one of his lectures right now. For once, I'd like not to be told how I could have handled things better. But then I focused on Violet, so small and fragile in my arms, that I couldn't bring myself to let her go and do the needful.

That's how I ended up here. With a sixty-year-old man stammering empty apologies behind me, and an angel in my lap.

"I thought you were just shy…" Uncle Fred's voice is flatter than I've ever heard it. He really does sound shaken, weirdly. This is all so surreal, I can't tell if I'm dreaming it.

"Your mother told me to kick you out," he says, in that same unfamiliar monotone.

Violet stirs in my arms, hanging onto me even more firmly. Even if I was planning on getting up, it's clear that she has no intention of letting go.

"I told her to go fuck herself. Excuse my language, dear," he carries on.

"That's cool. I believe I might have said something in a similar vein, earlier," Violet remarks.

I frown.

"Aye." Uncle Fred chuckles softly. "She really didn't appreciate that either."

"Hang on, what?" I ask, loosening my embrace and glancing at Violet. She's pressing her lips together tightly, but the creasing in the corner of her tear-filled eyes betrays her conflicting feelings.

She lets go of my neck and cups my face, wiping the wetness off my cheeks with her thumbs.

"I'm sorry, Chris. I don't think your mom is going

to approve of our relationship."

Uncle Fred chuckles again, more loudly. Though not nearly as loud as the blood rushing in my ears and my heart, racing in my chest.

"You told her *what* exactly?" I ask.

Her expression tenses, and she remains silent. I turn to look at Uncle Fred, who shrugs sheepishly. Then back at Violet, who's biting down hard on her bottom lip.

"I… kinda told her she was a monster who should rot in prison…" she whispers.

Uncle Fred clears his throat behind me, but doesn't interject.

"I see…" I mumble.

"I'm so sorry if I overstepped." Her eyes are wide with concern.

Sorry? She's seriously apologizing right now? For defending me? That's ludicrous. It's the most amazing thing to have ever happened to me. Outside of all the other amazing things that she's already done for me since yesterday.

"You said that?" I ask.

She's chewing on her lip again and I can't stand it. I can't stand any of what's been going on this morning, but this is something else.

I stare at her, waiting for her eyes to meet mine again. And when they do, and I still spot the tears in them, I take a deep breath and get over myself already. She made good on her promises. She followed me into my own personal hell and fought for me. And what did I do? I made a scene downstairs, and then another one up here in front of her. I've been feeling so damn sorry for myself that I didn't recognize my blessings.

The cheap gin I found under the bed still burns in the back of my throat. I shove the bottle aside, rolling it back out of sight where it belongs, and cup her pretty little face with both hands. How small and vulnerable she looks now. Hell, compared to me, she always looked comically tiny. Like a baby bird that needs my protection. Except, this baby bird is secretly a mighty eagle, claws and all.

"If anyone should apologize, it's me," I say.

She sniffles once and shakes her head. "No, you don't."

"Violet… I don't know how I'll ever repay you for everything you've done for me, but I'll spend the rest of my life trying to figure it out."

Her lips part with a soft gasp. I silence it with my mouth, pressing myself against her to make my point. She tastes even sweeter than she did this morning.

Though the alcohol attempts to numb me, I can still feel her, breathing life into me. And my heart, which had tried to shrivel and hide ever since I entered this house, starts to wake with renewed purpose. I've shown her the worst of me. All the ugliness I've been desperate to hide and wish away. She's seen all there is to see of me. And she's still here.

With her arms and even her legs wrapped around me, and her hands soothing the marks on my shoulders, Violet has managed to catch me at the exact moment I slipped, just like she said she would. I'll love her for that until the day I die. It's all that and more which I try to express in this kiss we share. Slow, gentle, and oh so very sweet.

Hopefully she gets the message, because words certainly can't do it justice.

I pull away to stare into her eyes, at half mast and dreamy. *I love you…*

You don't belong here… And neither do I anymore. Surrounded by dusty remnants of the past, she's shown me a glimpse of a possible future. It's up to me to seize it now.

"I think we should go," I say.

Her eyes widen in recognition, but she doesn't say anything.

"Aye, probably for the best," Uncle Fred remarks behind me. "And you're probably going to need this."

He leans forward and hands me my shirt, which I'd unceremoniously dumped on the living room floor earlier. I grip the fabric, crunching it up between my fingers. Not my finest moment, that. Violet's hand on my cheek forces me to focus on her again.

"Son." Uncle Fred sighs and rests his hand on my shoulder. "I've been a fool. Blind to everything that's been going on in this family. Maybe one day you'll be able to forgive me."

His voice is distant, I'm so absorbed in the depths of Violet's gaze.

"It's okay, Chris," she mouths.

She's right. It is okay now. In a flurry of rage, I did the one thing I'd been most afraid of my entire life. I showed everyone, including her, my true self. And she's still here.

Uncle Fred clears his throat and wipes his palms on his trousers as he starts to get up. "If you still want his ashes tomorrow, you have my number."

"Yeah…" I mumble. "Thanks, Uncle Fred."

"I'm glad you came. Both of you," he says.

So am I. For the first time in what feels like forever, Violet cracks a smile at me, and my chest fills with lightness and relief. That's when I realize, I'm already smiling at her too.

CHAPTER TWELVE

It's been hard to swallow the lump in my throat ever since we left Chris' childhood home. I expected things to get ugly, but nothing could have prepared me for the reality of it all. The bus ride back towards Edinburgh Old Town passes without much conversation between us, that's how shaken I am. Still, every time I glance at him in the seat beside me, I marvel at how relaxed he looks. And every time his thumb brushes across my knuckles, my heart skips a beat, and a smile teases at the corner of his mouth.

How is this even possible after everything that he's been through this morning?

"I could cancel tonight, you know," I tell him. I haven't been keen on it, anyway.

He shakes his head. "No way. It's the whole reason you made this trip."

"Yeah, but—"

"She's a good friend, isn't she?"

I nod. "My only actual friend, since, you know… I just… I'd much rather spend time with you."

He guides my chin in his direction, allowing us to make eye contact. I lose myself in his eyes. The way he looks at me is everything. I don't know how I'll ever get enough.

"Can you bring a plus one?"

The corners of my mouth quiver at his suggestion. Really? Mr. Antisocial over here is volunteering to accompany me to an actual party where he doesn't know anyone but me?

"I don't see why not…" I mumble.

"That way we can still spend time together, plus I get to make good on my part of the arrangement," he speaks resolutely. Like he's making a pledge.

I wrinkle my nose. "Arrangement. That's such a formal word." Also, we literally never discussed this. It did occur to me, though. How sad it would be to turn up to a celebration of love all alone and dateless. How great it would be to be able to bring someone.

He smiles briefly. "What would you prefer? Tit for tat?"

"Ugh, that's even worse!" I complain.

"Okay, how about I'm looking forward to the food? It's at a fancy restaurant, right? Perhaps it's about time I get out there and expand my palate beyond takeout."

That at last makes me chuckle, and I adore him for it. Because it's bullshit and we both know it. We haven't discussed it as such, but it's been pretty obvious that he has hang ups about food. And now he's supposedly looking forward to eating out at a high end restaurant? He's still looking out for me, despite going through his own personal hell this morning. What did I ever do to deserve a guy like him? I must be the luckiest girl in the world.

"Fine, I'll ask her!" I say, grinning up at him.

"Good!" he counters.

I squeeze his hand, and he squeezes it back like clockwork.

It's actually a huge relief to be able to bring a date to Irina's engagement party. I'd dreaded this moment. After the six months of heartache I've been through, it just seemed like too much of a stretch to be able to genuinely celebrate another couple's happiness. Add in the fact that Irina, Joyce, and I were so close for the three years we lived together. We were meant to be sisters. Seeing her is bound to drag up those same feelings of betrayal I've been battling ever since I found Joyce and Sam in bed together. And it's going to make me wonder all over again if our friendship was ever real at all. And by extension, whether Irina knew about what happened back then. I never mustered the courage to ask her or even talk about any of that with her; I've literally been avoiding her as well as everyone else in my life for six whole months.

In the end, Irina guilt tripped me and told me that I was the only college friend who could make it, and she didn't want to celebrate without me. Blegh. Oh well, at least I can be sure I'm not about to run into Joyce.

But after how things have unfolded with Chris over the past 24 hours, my feelings have shifted. Now I *can* celebrate love. At least I'm starting to believe in the concept again. Because I guess that's what this is. Or the beginnings of it. I was ready to follow him to a literal funeral, what's a dinner hosted by an old friend in comparison? Nothing. It's actually nothing. And now, I'll have him right there by my side throughout.

Chris tenses beside me and lets go of my hand to hit the button signaling the bus to stop.

"Are we here already?" I ask, peering out the window. Our surroundings don't look right; they're run down, much rougher than the center of town.

"Not exactly, but there's something we should do before we head back to the room," he says.

"Okay…"

The bus rolls to a halt, and Chris' hand on my shoulder beckons me to get out of my seat. I'm not very familiar with this part of Edinburgh, but then I'm hardly a local.

"Where are we going?" I ask. My hand seeks out his again once we're standing on the pavement outside a row of what looks like abandoned office buildings.

"Just a little side quest." He glances down at me

and gently squeezes my fingers. "Trust me?"

"Always," I say, which makes him smile, but only briefly. Maybe this is deeper than a so-called side quest.

He leads me down the street in the direction our bus just came from. The dark tinted windows and neon signs are of the usual type for this kind of area. Betting shops, adult entertainment, and a pub which looks like it's seen much better days.

Chris lets go of my hand and places his arm around my shoulder, and despite where we are, I couldn't possibly feel safer. This is what it must feel like to have a personal bodyguard.

A short walk later, we find ourselves outside a brightly lit up generic fried chicken place, and I finally get it. He's on a trip down memory lane.

Chris pauses to look at me, then through the taped up broken windowpane of the shop, then back at me.

"This might have been a dumb idea," he mumbles.

I shake my head. No, it wasn't. This is perfect. "You know what? I'm starving, actually."

He exhales sharply and pushes the door open for me. The customary chime alerts the young Asian guy with the sharply styled beard and fade behind the counter.

"Hey, what can I get you?" he asks.

I look up at Chris. "The usual?"

He nods. "Yeah, a big bucket meal, please." Then

he glances at the group of vaping teenagers occupying the two tables in the corner, who all turned around to size us up the moment we walked in. "Take away."

"Aight." The guy behind the counter rings up our order, and Chris makes the payment in silence. By then, the kids are back to their trays of greasy food and loud banter.

"It's nothing special, but…" Chris tells me under his breath, barely audible over the rattling exhaust fan above the deep fat fryer.

"Fried chicken is good with me," I tell him. Even if it wasn't, I love that he brought me here. The moment I read the sign, I understood. This is where he used to go with his dad. Fried chicken makes for a sorry consolation for all the shit he went through at home, but in hindsight, it's the closest he might have to a happy childhood memory.

I rest my hand on his upper arm while we wait for our food. Luckily, it doesn't take all that long, because I can feel the tension build between us. Perhaps the smell of stale oil is getting to my head as well.

We watch while our food is packed up in a flimsy paper bag. Finally, the lad turns around and places it on the counter. Not a moment too soon, since I'm getting pretty light-headed. "Help yourself to two drinks," he says, nodding at the glass-front fridge next to us. The door is covered in greasy fingerprints, but I pretend not to notice.

"Chris?" I ask.

"Uhh… I'll have a Coke," he says.

I take out two Cokes and nudge the sticky door shut with my elbow. Chris picks up the bag and opens the door for me, then follows. It chimes again as it closes behind us.

I take in a lung full of fresh air and feel better already. That was weird. I'm not normally this sensitive to smells. This morning has been a lot. And probably that sip of mystery booze I downed in Chris' room earlier is having a rave in my otherwise empty stomach.

"It's dirtier than I remember," Chris mumbles. "I'm sorry. We can just go eat someplace else."

"No way, I really am starving." I smile up at him. When he reciprocates, all is right in the world again. Sort of.

We make our way back to the bus stop and sit on the bench. I gesture at the greasy bag. "Just a little taste 'til our bus gets here."

He suppresses a grin and holds it up in my direction. Now that we're out in the open, the food actually smells quite tempting. Certainly better than a certain chain restaurant we've all heard of. I use the first of the stack of paper napkins to wipe my hands before selecting a juicy looking leg piece.

"Oh, it's spicy," I comment, after taking my first bite. "Nice!"

"Yeah, they add their own mix on top which gives it a little kick," Chris says, picking up a piece for himself as well.

I lean back against the bench and savor my crispy fried chicken. In hindsight I wasn't lying when I told him I'm starving. And honestly, even if it sucked, I would never admit it to him. Not today and not ever.

"So, you used to come here together?" I ask.

He nods. "All the time."

I try not to dwell on what's left unsaid. If his dad took him out for fried chicken every time he got a beating, then…Ugh. I hate that he's trying to share a piece of himself with me, and that's all I can think about.

"It's okay if you don't like it, we can get something—"

"It's not that, I'm just…" I look up at him and suddenly don't know how to complete that sentence anymore.

"I'm really sorry about what happened back there," he whispers.

I shake my head and force a smile. "Not your fault. I just feel so bad about everything you had to go through."

"Likewise, that's not your fault," he says.

How did he go through all that shit and still turn out so amazing? There will never come a time that I won't be in absolute awe of this man.

"Too bad we can't change the past, huh?" I ask. I certainly know what I'd go back and change if I only could.

"Only the present and future," he remarks.

That's a lovely thought. He's lovely all over. And what's even better is that I'm here with him, and he's here with me. This is the future I would like to work towards.

"I'm so glad we're not pretending anymore," I breathe.

"You know, I was always quite shit at pretending," he replies. Chris wraps his half-eaten piece of chicken in a napkin, and puts it back in the bag before gently placing his clean hand on my cheek. I follow his example and turn to face him, resting my hand on top of his.

"Yeah… same here." I take a deep breath and keep staring into those endlessly blue eyes of his. "You know, I lov—"

Just at that moment, a loud squeal and hiss signals our bus' arrival and the spell is broken. This isn't the time and place. The first time I tell him what I'm about to say needs to be somewhere better than the graffitied bus stop near his dead dad's go-to fried chicken joint. It needs to be somewhere fresh and new, not on the way home from a funeral, weighed down by emotional baggage and childhood trauma.

We jump up and rush to gather our lunch before

getting on the bus. Once we're settled in our extra legroom seats, Chris turns to me with a puzzled expression on his face.

"You were saying?"

"I was saying I really love the chicken…" I say, adding: "Just not as much as last night's takeout pizza."

He lets out a hearty chuckle and wraps his arm around me, allowing me to rest my head against his chest while I try and breathe. It's unnerving how close I came to confessing my feelings to him. After, what, barely 24 hours? There's so much we don't know about each other yet. So much we still have to discover. How can I be this certain this quickly? It's got to be a side effect of emotions running high all morning! And even if my feelings are true, this declaration is bound to freak him out, so I should probably take a step or two back. We agreed to take things slow, after all.

We sit like this in silence for a few minutes, until he clears his throat. "So, this party, just how fancy do you think it will be?"

I exhale sharply and shrug. "No idea exactly."

"Is there a dress code?" he asks, while running his finger halfway down his shirt, past the spot that's missing a button.

"We still have time to sort something out," I reassure him. "After we enjoy our lunch."

He smiles briefly, then trains his eyes on the cityscape passing us by outside the window.

Looking forward to expanding his palate, my ass. He's nervous about tonight. He's just too much of a gentleman to let me know.

CHAPTER THIRTEEN

*** Chris ***

Violet is a superhero. Her super power? Problem solving and spreading a sense of zen wherever she goes. The more I think about it, the more certain I am of it.

With the subtlest of smiles, the briefest touch—with her sheer presence—she manages to calm even the worst of my fears. All without making me feel like a worthless shit in comparison, somehow. I don't know how she does it.

We reach the Airbnb, share the rest of that chicken bucket, locate a big and tall menswear shop nearby, pick out a new shirt for me to wear, each have a shower, and get dressed, all with enough time for a breather before we head off to her friend's party. Whom she called at some point in between all of this to confirm that she's bringing a date.

On my own, I would have quickly gotten overwhelmed and judged all of this impossible.

And yet... She hasn't even broken a sweat by the time she comes out of the bathroom. Her hair and makeup is done up like she belongs in a fashion magazine. And all those curves I can't stop visualizing whenever I close my eyes are tastefully highlighted by the light pink cable-knit dress she's wearing. Her favorite color is about to become mine too. She just looks so damn good in it!

"Wow." That's all I can say. All I can think. I get up off the bed and take a few steps in her direction.

"Wow, yourself." She smiles brightly when she approaches me the rest of the way. Her fingertips dance playfully across the collar of my new shirt, taking my breath away. Crisp and white. Though I wasn't sure about it, she insisted. But once I put it on, I realized that she was right. It combines very well with the only pair of jeans I carried on this trip.

She takes my left arm, and unbuttons the cuff of the shirt. I swallow the urge to protest.

"Trust me?" she asks.

I nod and watch as she folds the sleeve over a couple of times. Then, she repeats the process on the other side. Although I don't have too many scars on my lower arms, there are a couple. They stand out angrily against my relatively light skin.

"You look good enough to eat, Chris," she says.

I swallow further protest, because that can't be right.

"So do you…" I mumble.

She smiles, which looks even more radiant

outlined in red lipstick.

"I'd be tempted to try, but then I'd have to do my make-up all over again," she teases. "Maybe later, huh?"

Just like that, I've got imagery in my head which is going to make it impossible to act cool. I'm regretting everything I said about tagging along. There's no way I'm getting through the evening without making a fool of myself. Not just in front of her, but her friends as well.

"Chris…" She rests her hand on the bare skin on my forearm. It still stings, but in a pleasant way. "I'm so glad you're coming with me tonight. Thank you."

"Don't worry about it," I say. I want to add a clever remark about our arrangement, but I'm not feeling witty enough right now. I'm just…

I'm fucking horny, is what I am. Ever since we reached this place last night, we've spent the majority of our time with our hands all over each other. Well, almost all over. We kissed until our lips turned raw, cuddled and caressed each other, even fell asleep in each other's arms for hours on end. The only reason we didn't go any further than that was me and my stupid, stupid hang-ups. Our chemistry is so insanely strong, we even kissed in front of Uncle Fred, on the floor of my old room, while I was still crying like a little bitch.

And now we're heading out together, in polite

company. With her looking pretty as a picture, and me… me…

Sporting the most persistent and painful erection of my entire life. Despite being too damn busy all afternoon to get handsy with her. If anything, that little bit of distance between us has made me crave her even more.

And sweet Violet, she has no idea. I started off so terrified of opening up to her that I never considered this potential outcome of us 'taking things slow.' I need release; I need to take the edge off so bad, I can hardly think of anything else.

"Are you okay?" she asks.

Sweet baby girl, you have no idea right now.

I nod briefly. "I'm good."

"Cool, so I can book the cab?" She holds up her phone.

"Just a sec, I'll be all set in a minute," I tell her, while making my way back towards the bathroom.

"Okay!"

I close the door behind me and lean against it, trying to catch a breath. When I close my eyes, images of Violet's lusciously painted lips flood my mind. Good enough to eat, she said? *Holy shit.*

I hurriedly slip my hand into my jeans, feeling myself. This won't take long. Not long at all…

That dress she's wearing really shows off all her best assets. But even otherwise. I remember feeling her weigh down on my crotch when she straddled me last night. And then again earlier today… Her hands all over my bare shoulders and back, touching me without a care in the world.

Apparently, people just do that. They touch each other without worrying about whether they're doing the right thing… Like when I gripped her hips last night. Fighting every last ounce of my self control not to grind myself to a messy finale against her.

Shit, we were so busy all afternoon preparing for this party, we didn't really do anything beyond that kiss in my old room. And still… Every time she looked in my direction on the bus. Every time I put my arm around her or touched her hand, I felt that same electricity, that same magnetic pull. I kept on wanting to touch her again and again and again.

What would it feel like to have her touch me like this? Her sweet, slender fingers tightening around something other than my hand or arm or shoulder?

I'm working myself pretty hard now, palming my cock, trying to force a quick climax before she gets suspicious. That's when I open my eyes, catching a glimpse of myself in the mirror. Red-faced and red-handed. I'm horrified by my own reflection.

Violet's baby pink toiletry bag on the counter, and unicorn pajamas hanging from the towel rack only deepen my regret. I can't do this. I can't jerk myself off to fantasies of her, only to clean up the evidence and pretend like it didn't happen. With her just on the other side of that door. It's wrong. Am I really going to act like I'm some respectable guy deserving to accompany her to her friend's engagement party after all this? I'm rather shit at pretending anyway. I'm never going to convince anyone, least of all myself.

She'll see right through me.

I rush to the sink and fully open the cold tap. The water is so chilly, it stings. I splash some in my face, then pause with my hands underneath the stream until they go numb. A few deep breaths later, I can finally look myself in the eye again.

This is not happening. I'm not going to do this in secret. We're going to go to this party as planned, and then…

Then… If all goes well, and I haven't made an arse of myself—If I've *earned* it, we'll come back here together, and then I'll handle this like a man. If we end up kissing and cuddling and doing all those amazing things we did yesterday evening, then I'll make my desires known.

Before the end of the night, I'll simply tell her. Or I'll show her. Or something.

I want her. I've wanted her right from the start, but I was just too much of a coward to let it happen before. I won't make that same mistake again.

*** Violet ***

Chris looks flustered throughout our Uber ride to the party. He's nervous, poor guy. Last time I proposed to cancel didn't go so well, which stops me from asking again if he's changed his mind.

It'll be fine, I try to tell myself. Once we get there, and we get the introductions and initial small talk out of the way, we can just focus on each other again. All will be okay then. We're good together. We're going to be good together, even in a crowd.

"This is it," the driver announces, as we pull up outside a row of Victorian brick buildings.

"Thanks!" I squeeze Chris' hand, and he squeezes it back while forcing a smile.

"They won't bite," I tell him under my breath.

"Heh, yeah."

It's already dark, and more than a little windy and cold. The outside of our destination is tastefully lit up with old fashioned lanterns, inviting the eye towards the sign which reads: 'Just Fish. By Callum Byrne.'

I've heard that name somewhere before. Is he some kind of famous person?

I tuck my hand into the crook of Chris' arm once

we get out of the car and walk towards the entrance. It's a relatively new place; I don't recall it being here back when I still lived in the city.

"Fancy indeed," Chris mumbles. Meanwhile, I give my name to the smartly dressed host, who leads us through the main area of the restaurant and into a function room at the back. Irina and a handful of others are already there.

"Hey! I hope we're not late," I greet her with my arms stretched out.

"Violet, oh my god, you made it!" she squeals, rushing towards me to give me a big hug. "I've missed you so much, girl!"

I hug her back tightly, while forcing out a mumbled congratulations past the lump growing in the back of my throat. Guilt laced with a sprinkling of betrayal? I'm not sure how to identify this feeling.

"Thanks! So, you've got to meet Matt," she says. "And remember my mom?"

I straighten myself and take a deep breath "Hello, Mrs. Kowalczyk." I wave at the only person over fifty-five in the room—Irina's mom, who nods and smiles at me.

The similarities between the two are striking. The same long blonde hair, similar athletic build, and friendly smile. I've only met her once before, when Irina and I decided to backpack through continental Europe one summer and made a short stop at her childhood home in Poland.

Irina turns around and waves at her fiancé to come over and meet us. At six feet tall and on the huskier side of the spectrum, Matt projects friendly protector vibes, but he's no Chris. Still, he's quite different from the sort of guys Irina used to date. Rather, the sort of guys both of us used to date. It's a pleasant surprise, and I like him immediately.

"Hi, Matt," I say, while shaking his hand. It's warm and reassuring. A good, strong handshake. "Congratulations to you too!"

"So, Irina, this is Chris, my d—" I grab Chris by the arm and coax him closer to me, "—my boyfriend."

I glance up at him and find him staring at me in surprise, before smiling at Irina.

"This is Irina, my college bestie," I tell him. "And her fiancé, Matt."

"Nice to meet you both. Congrats," Chris says.

"Nice to meet you too, Chris." Irina smiles up at him when they shake hands, then trains her gaze on me again. "We have a lot of catching up to do, you and I."

I press my lips together and shrug. "Yeah, it's been a while… But first, you two. How did this happen all of a sudden? I didn't even know you were dating anyone!"

Irina leans into Matt, who sweetly puts his arm

around her and smiles. "It's quite the story," she says. "I'll tell you all about it over dinner."

I glance up at Chris, who is staring at me pretty intensely again. *Boyfriend.* I love how much easier the word rolls off my tongue now. Does he like it as much? Introducing him as such was a test, I'll admit. Sure, he introduced me to his family as his girlfriend, but that was different, somehow. That was part of our old plan of pretense. This feels more real. But certainly safer than blurting out the L-word out of the blue.

"And how about you guys?" Irina asks. "First you RSVP for one, and then…"

"I hope I'm not intruding," Chris interjects.

"Absolutely not, the more the merrier!" Irina says. "I always said to bring someone." She gives me a look. One of those that speaks a thousand words. Because her initial invitation included… Sam. And I couldn't decide whether she seriously didn't know what had happened, or if she was provoking me into telling her about it. Then again, I've always known her to be a straightforward person. It would have been unlike her to play such mind games.

"Anyway… Is there a seating plan?" I ask.

Chris rests his hand on my shoulder, which allows me to breathe freely again.

"Nah, just sit wherever you like," Irina says. "We're just waiting for a couple more people and then they'll start serving the food."

I nod, and reach for Chris' hand on me.

He leans down in my direction. "Do you know anyone else here?"

I shake my head. We circle the room, introducing ourselves as Irina's college roommate, and boyfriend. And every time I say it, it becomes a little easier. Even Chris is starting to look more at ease now, standing proud and confident while making small talk with some of Irina's colleagues and casual friends. I guess my gamble paid off.

We meet everyone up close, including Irina's mom, who we try but fail to have a little chat with. Her broken English and what little German I remember from school doesn't really suffice and she soon excuses herself to go to the ladies' room, leaving us alone for a moment.

"Boyfriend, huh?" he asks, a smile playing on his lips.

I look up at him. "Is that okay?"

"Yeah, I mean…" He sighs deeply. "I already told everyone back home that you're my girlfriend…"

"Exactly."

"But that was different, wasn't it?" he says.

"I suppose. It was different, but it's also kind of the same, right?" I ask.

He looks down at me, his eyebrows slightly raised in wonder. "I've never been introduced as anyone's boyfriend before."

"There's a first time for everything." I grin.

The more I look at him, the more I want to kiss him. That wouldn't be a problem, and I'm certainly not shy about public displays of affection, except… Once I kiss him, I'm going to want to touch him. And once I touch him, I'm going to want so much more. I've had a very hard time getting my desires under control since last night. And this isn't the time or place for any of that. Plus, we're meant to be taking things slow.

I get up on my tippy toes and steal a quick and rather tame peck on the lips. Which turns them red. Oops.

"Heh, you've got some lipstick on you," I say, while trying to wipe it off with my thumb.

He grins at me. "Oh well, in that case, I guess we match."

That makes me laugh out loud. Until… I hear a familiar voice behind me, which chokes the sound out of my throat.

"Irina, sweetie! Congratulations!"

"Joyce, so happy you could come!" Irina says.

My knees suddenly turn to jelly, causing my legs to tremble. This was not supposed to happen.

"Violet, are you okay?" Chris asks me. Both his hands on my upper arms seek to steady me, but I'm unable to answer.

"I…"

"Please, sit," he suggests, pulling out a couple of chairs for us.

I can't quite catch a deep enough breath, and the room is starting to spin. My limbs grow impossibly heavy and my vision turns blurry. Chris' firm grip on my arms guides me onto the chair, and I sink into the backrest while my heart races out of control.

He leans in, squeezing my shoulder and rubbing my hand. All the while, gazing into my eyes with a concerned frown on his face. That's what I try to focus on. All of it.

His rhythmically calming touch, his beautiful blue eyes, and his lips, moving steadily while he tries to reassure me. Even if I can't comprehend his words right now, I know they're good. I know he's good. I know I'm safe, because he's here with me. Even though my body is fighting me, I force myself to breathe deeper, and calmer.

"She wasn't supposed to be here," I stammer, once I'm able.

"No… No, she wasn't," he says.

"Is she—" I swallow hard. "Is she alone?"

Chris turns around, but his hand never leaves mine.

"Hey, Violet, what happened?" another voice asks. It's one of the colleagues I'd said hello to earlier. "Shall I get you some water?"

I blink at her and shake my head, then turn to Chris, who's focusing on me again. "Is she?"

He slowly shakes his head. "No. She's not."

At that very moment, I hear his voice. His stupid, arrogant voice, offering half-hearted best wishes to Irina and Matt. And something snaps in me.

"Okay…" I mumble and take a deep breath, before straightening myself against the backrest. "Fuck it."

"What are you—" Chris says.

"Something I should have done months ago."

I ball my fists and get up, crossing the room in a few long strides.

"Joyce, Sam, what an unexpected pleasure to see you here," I say. "And thanks for the surprise, Irina!"

The three of them turn around to face me. And the only one who dares look at me straight is Irina. Her eyes are wide with shock, while Joyce and Sam are avoiding my gaze completely.

"I…" Irina stammers. "I didn't know."

I shake my head. "You said she wasn't coming."

Joyce scoffs. "That's what she told me too, or I would've backed out."

I glare at her. "You don't get to talk to me."

Sam huffs. "Calm down, Violet. We're all consenting adults here. Just get over it already."

I size him up. "Get over it? Okay, that's cool, Sam. Why don't you tell everyone what exactly I'm supposed to get over, in your own words."

Irina looks like she's about to cry. Matt joins her side and puts his arm around her protectively, while staring down the rest of us. Luckily for him, he doesn't say anything. This might be her big celebration, but I can't muster the energy to care about that. I'm ready to burn any bridge that gets in my way now.

"Don't be a child," Sam grumbles.

"Joyce… Maybe you care to explain the situation?" I ask.

"You just weren't compatible." She shrugs. "That's hardly my fault."

"Okay." I feel a warm presence behind me. I don't even need to turn around to know that it's Chris, because his hand ends up on the small of my back as if to say: *I'm here. Say what you need to say.*

Funny how life comes full circle sometimes. That's exactly what I told him earlier today when he faced down his own mother.

"Here's the deal," I tell Irina. "Six months ago, I was heading out to do a big project on the other side of London. I was supposed to be out all day, but I had to turn back, because I'd forgotten my sketchbook. Imagine my surprise when I unlock my front door and find not only that Sam hasn't gone to the job interview he said he'd lined up that morning, but Joyce is there too."

Sam exhales sharply through his teeth.

"A coincidence, one might think, if not for the fact that both of them were buck naked, and she had his dick in her mouth!"

Irina gasps and covers her mouth.

"That's not…" Joyce stammers. "It's really not that simple."

"No?"

"You and Sam had been having some problems… You weren't happy, you even told me so," she says, while looking to Irina for support. "Meanwhile, Sam and I fell in love, is that so bad?"

Irina just blinks at her, but doesn't comment.

"Yeah, wanna know why we were having problems?" I ask. "Because Sam would spend more time going out with the boys or playing on his phone than actually being a supposed grown-up and having real grown-up conversations with me."

"It takes two to tango. You can't just blame everything on him," Joyce argues. "You two just didn't belong together."

"Maybe not, but then again, that could have been discussed. We could have talked about it and gone our separate ways. What I can't abide by is the fact that you two had been fucking behind my back for who knows how long! In my bed! In the flat I fucking paid for!" I rant.

Chris' hand on my back continues to give me

strength. For six months I'd been thinking about a scenario like this, a chance to confront either one of them and say my piece. And I always concluded it would go badly. I'd be a blubbering mess; I wouldn't be able to get my point across and then I'd kick myself later once I figured out exactly what to say.

This is not that. This is my moment.

"He was depressed, because he'd been having trouble finding a job since getting laid off," Joyce explains.

"Sure. Why not? And that gives him the right to cheat. What's your excuse?" I say.

Irina clears her throat, and all eyes are on her all of a sudden. "I…"

She looks at me with big tear-filled eyes, then at Joyce. "I want you to leave."

"Okay," I say. Good riddance. I should have just stayed home with Chris like I wanted to, anyway.

"No, not you, Violet," she says. "Joyce and Sam, get the fuck out."

"But… We're supposed to be besties!" Joyce complains. "All's fair in love and war; isn't that what they say? How is any of this my fault?"

I glance over at Sam, who is standing just a couple of feet outside all of the commotion, his hands buried deep in his pockets. I can't believe I used to find this little weasel attractive. All of this is happening because of him, and he can't even back up his girl. What a coward. I'm outraged on her behalf, almost, but then. They fucking deserve each other.

"I'm sure that's exactly what he will tell you later on when you find out about the side chicks he's cheating on you with," I tell her.

Sam glares at me. Probably because I'm spot on. "Come on, let's go," he tells Joyce.

"But…" Joyce is literally pouting like a child when she looks at Irina again.

"Let's. Go," he repeats, while pointing at the door. Nobody says another word while the two of them leave in silence.

"Violet…" Irina says, taking a step in my direction.

I glance at her, but adrenaline is still coursing through me, keeping me on edge.

"I had no idea. I'm so very sorry." She reaches for my arm.

I try to breathe, to calm down. Chris' hand creeps up my back and ends up on my shoulder, squeezing it gently as if to remind me that the fight is over. It's safe to retreat now.

"If I had known this is what happened, I would have never—" Tears are streaming down her face now. Matt looks concerned. Probably just about as concerned as how Chris must be looking at me right now. Funny. I guess we both learned the same lesson at roughly the same time. Bad boys aren't worth shit.

Irina's mom appears by her side, asking a million

questions a minute. I can't understand a word, so I wait for the two of them to finish their exchange before answering.

"It's not like I told you anything. How could you know?" I say, finally.

"I thought it was weird that you stopped taking my calls. Joyce had stopped talking to me a couple of months earlier… I felt like our group was falling apart and I had to bring us all back together somehow," Irina says.

I close my eyes and try to breathe through the tension locked in my chest. I can't blame her. She's always been the mediator of the group, making sure nobody ever felt left out, which is quite a feat in a group of three. I lean back against Chris, who continues to give me strength.

Funny. We're here together because I offered to be *his* backup. I never imagined that I'd need him to return the favor the very same evening. He caught me just now. This is what a relationship should be.

When I open my eyes and look at Irina again, I feel lighter. I feel vindicated. With Chris backing me up, I can leave the last six months behind and look forward. We can't change the past, only the present and future. And the prospect of a future with him makes me smile.

"Not your fault. You couldn't know. I was so hurt after everything that I didn't know how to—"

"I wish you'd told me, but I understand why you didn't," Irina whispers.

I stretch my arms out in her direction, and she does the same. Moments later, we're hugging each other and apologizing over and over.

I'm the one to pull back first, and spot a very awkward looking Matt behind her, still standing guard with a bewildered look in his eyes.

Turning around, I see Chris, his hands buried deep in his pockets, with that same puppy dog stare. And that's enough to set me off.

It starts with a chuckle, and soon turns into a giggle.

"Oh my god, look at the two of you!" I say.

Irina dabs at her eyes with the back of her hand and follows my gaze. "You know what, Violet," she tells me.

"Mhm?" I mumble, while trying to get my laughter under control.

"I think we both did amazingly well, actually." She smiles up at Matt.

"Oh, for sure!" I say. "We got super lucky."

"I can't wait for you to tell me all about it." Irina takes my hand and squeezes it.

"Right, I think that's more than enough drama for one night," Matt grumbles. "What do you say, let's leave the girls to catch up?"

Chris nods stoically. "Sure thing, mate."

The two of them wander off and take a seat at the beautifully laid out table. Oh crap, yes. This is supposed to be an engagement party, which Joyce and I turned into a shouting match. How embarrassing.

"I'm sorry to make a scene, messing up your engagement party," I tell Irina.

"Oh, nothing's messed up! This party is happening no matter what." She grins.

I smile back at her. The blotches of mascara underneath her eyes remind me that my makeup is probably in a similar sorry state.

"Hey, perhaps we should freshen up?" I suggest.

She glances at Matt, who is already engaged in conversation with Chris, before grabbing her handbag. "Excellent idea."

We're arm in arm, heading to the ladies' room. Irina signals to one of the waiters on the way to start serving the food. Once we find ourselves alone in front of the mirrored wall, I can no longer contain my curiosity.

"So, Matt… How did that happen?"

"Oh it's a crazy story. How about Chris?"

I chuckle. "The craziest. You go first."

She takes out a packet of makeup wipes from her bag and hands me one. "Remember a few months ago there was that virus scare in Paris?"

"Uhh…" I frown. "Vaguely. Didn't that turn out to be a hoax, though?"

"Well, they took it extremely seriously at the time. Put me in quarantine for two weeks on my stopover."

"What?!"

"Right, that's what I thought. Anyway, long story short, I was getting a serious case of cabin fever after a couple of days and was desperate to talk to literally anyone, so I started calling the other rooms in the hotel."

"Shit, you could have just called me! I wasn't in a good headspace, but if I'd known you were stranded all by yourself—" I say.

"I would have totally tried that, except I'd smashed up my phone on the way to the airport, so I was stuck with the hotel phone, and that seemed to be on some weird intercom system."

I forget entirely what we're both here for and just stand there listening to her insane story, holding the makeup wipe in my hand, while she fixes her mascara and lipstick. She literally met Matt over the phone in that hotel, and they got along so well that she simply had to have him once the quarantine period was over. Holy shit.

"You weren't exaggerating, that's crazy!" I mumble.

She checks herself out in the mirror once more, before smiling at me. "Your turn. What's the deal with you and Chris?"

"Chris… He's just…" I catch myself blushing

while staring at the makeup wipe in my hand. "Even I can hardly believe it when I think about it, but we literally met on the train over here."

She gasps. "No way! You seem so… You guys are adorable together!"

"Right? That's how I feel too."

"So you met yesterday on the train, and then?" she asks.

"We were just making small talk, right? And I asked him what brought him to Edinburgh, and he told me he was going to his dad's funeral…. But maybe don't mention I told you this, okay? It's an understandably raw topic for him."

She's full-on gaping at me now, but nods briefly.

"So, he was having a really hard time with it and he seemed like such a sweet guy that I said, why don't I tag along for emotional support?"

"You didn't!"

"I did. This morning," I say.

"Not an ideal first date, I imagine."

"Yeah, not at all. That's why we had our first date last night. Takeout from Luciano's on the way to that loft which I painted near the Royal Mile. Remember that place?"

"How could I forget, that mural is still my favorite. But… that's like, a studio flat."

"It is."

"With just one double bed."

"Yep." I nod solemnly.

"Violet, you didn't! Not on the first date, surely?" She grins at me while wiggling her eyebrows.

"I would never!" I tell her. Except, I totally would have. "We're taking things slow."

"Uh-huh. Well, you're super cute together. I wouldn't have guessed that you only just met. The way he looks at you is literally the sweetest thing."

"Yeah… I think…" I let my voice trail off rather than completing my thought.

"He's the one?" she asks, with a knowing smile playing on her lips.

"When did you know, with Matt?"

She shrugs. "Oh, after a few days."

"A few days after you met in person?" I ask.

She shakes her head and smiles. Which makes me smile too, because I completely understand.

"When you know, you know," she says. "I don't think timelines matter."

"Yeah… Me neither."

She playfully bumps me in the arm with her elbow. "Now fix your face already, they must have served the starters by now!"

"Yes ma'am!" I tease, while quickly tidying up my lower lash line and throwing the used wipe in the trash. That'll do.

CHAPTER FIFTEEN

* Chris *

Despite the rather dramatic start to the evening, the party turned out more fun than I expected. Everyone was friendly and easy to talk to, and the food was okay too.

What am I saying? The food was amazing.

Better still, nobody stared or looked at me funny throughout. As Violet's boyfriend, I was just one of them. Invited, accepted, even appreciated. I guess this is what life is like for normal people. They can just meet a few friends for a meal, and have fun without reading too much into it. But for me, the engagement party I offered to attend simply to support Violet started a revelation. A glimpse into a different life than the one I'd been living so far.

There's just one problem, which I couldn't stop obsessing about once we were alone again.

Sam.

He served as a stark reminder that maybe reality isn't exactly black and white. It's neither the shit show of my childhood, which I'd tried so hard to run away from, nor is it a blissful dream. There's always going to be good and bad stuff, it's just the proportion that differs. And sometimes, things get thrown out of balance without anyone noticing until it's too late.

Sounds like that's what happened with Violet and Sam.

They must have been happy at one point, until suddenly, they weren't anymore, so he cheated. When I saw him, I was enraged. All I could think about was how he shattered her heart. It took every bit of my self control to stand there behind Violet and let her handle the situation her way. Had I snapped, I would have taken matters in a very different direction than she did. I wanted to smash his smug face into the wall, honestly.

But in hindsight, there's something else in my heart. Not just anger for what he did to her, but something much more insidious. And that's what had me rushing into the bathroom as soon as we arrived back at the Airbnb. Where I still am, almost ten minutes later.

Meeting Sam was like peering into a magic mirror. Because he's my opposite in so many ways, it unnerves me now, thinking back.

At six feet tall, with broad, muscular shoulders and arms and perfectly flat abs, he looked like he belonged on a magazine cover rather than the real world. The only similarities we share are that we both have a beard and blue eyes. That's it.

He's the physical ideal, and I'm the consolation

prize. And that's what I can't stop thinking about. And I'm furious, not just at him, but at myself too. God, I'm jealous like I've never been. Had I won the genetic lottery like him, I still would have considered myself lucky to end up with a woman like Violet. I certainly would never have squandered my chance with her.

There's a knock on the door, which makes me tense up.

"Are you okay?" Violet asks.

"Yeah, just a minute," I tell her.

It's a lie. I'm not okay.

The last time I was here, compulsively dousing my hands and face in cold water, feels like an eternity ago. Back then I had a very different problem. Although that's not true either. The old problem never went away. I still want her so much it hurts.

But back then I'd almost convinced myself I had a chance at getting it. Now, I'm painfully aware of just how much I don't deserve her. I close my eyes and try to recapture that old feeling.

All night, I couldn't stop looking at her, kept craving even a hint of a smile or the briefest of touches. And she delivered every step of the way. Often she was already looking at me too. Already reaching for me. Already *there*, sporting that same look in her eye as last night when she climbed me on the sofa.

But was all that really for me? I found it hard to believe at the time, despite her protests. She might not realize it herself, but perhaps she's simply projecting old desires onto me, because the one she really wanted betrayed her? That might explain a few things.

"Okay, Chris, please will you talk to me?" Violet says.

I sigh deeply and shake my head. So much for seducing her tonight. After a whole evening of everything going splendidly in my favor, I'm making a fool of myself the second we're alone. All because I can't get my mind under control.

She might have changed my outlook on a lot of things since we met, but I'm still the same person. I'll still never be good enough. I'm not even sane right now.

When I finally unlock the door and push it open, I find her already waiting. Her head is cocked to the left, and her eyebrows are pulled together in concern.

"Violet…"

"Yeah?" How fragile she looks when those wide eyes of hers stare up at me. A part of me just wants to gather her up into my arms and never let go. Instead, I bury my hands deeply in my pockets. Probably because I know if I touch her right now, I won't be able to think straight anymore. I will never ask any of the questions I really need an answer to.

"Please tell me about you and Sam."

She frowns and shakes her head briefly. "Why? What good will it do?"

"I just… I need to know the whole story."

She nods at the sofa. "Sit with me?"

I follow her lead and end up next to her. She kicks her shoes off and puts her feet up on the sofa, wrapping her arms around her knees. That makes her look even smaller.

"We met at a pub… You probably know it—the White Hart, which is just around the corner from Teddington High Street?"

I nod. It's quite a historic place. I remember an article about it in the local paper a couple of months ago.

"I didn't know then what I know now. At the time, he seemed nice enough. A smooth talker; could speak endlessly about literally any topic. He knew how to chat himself up and make you trust him." Violet looks up at me and makes a face. "But it was an act, and actually he's a good-for-nothing fuck boy, who has no ambitions in life beyond mooching off as many women as possible. I must have been so naive not to see the red flags."

"What red flags?" I ask.

"How he always had an excuse for everything. He was late: there had been an accident on the way, or the bus broke down. He was broke: well, obviously he had to send money to his mom for some emergency or other, or someone had stolen his wallet. He couldn't find a job: the economy was crap and the girl at the Job Center hated him and wouldn't send him any good opportunities. It was always the same shit, and at first, I ate it up." Although she tries to shrug it off, I recognize the lingering embarrassment in her.

"When I caught on that he was just feeding me bullshit story after bullshit story, that's when our relationship soured."

Anger swells in my chest again. Violet is kind and helpful. She would have fallen for his nonsense, because she likes to see the best in people. That's literally the whole reason I'm here with her right now. As soon as I told her about where I was going, she just had to jump in to help.

"We argued a lot, and nothing would ever change. But because we'd already moved in together, it made sense to me to try and work things out. He claimed to be open to it, and made a big show of not wanting to lose me. I'm sure that's roughly when he started looking for his next mark, in hindsight. He was just buying time for himself, so he wouldn't be stuck without a place to stay."

That asshole took advantage of her good nature and kept stringing her along even after she caught onto his schemes. What an absolute dog.

I can't take it anymore and reach for Violet's hand.

She threads her fingers through mine, dulling the ache that's been developing in my heart ever since we left the restaurant. When she looks down at our intertwined hands, she tightens her grip on me. I might have forced this conversation, but perhaps she needed to express it. This is just another chance for me to help her how she helped me earlier today. I just wish… I wish this was more than that.

"When it happened, when I saw them together, reality seemed to implode. Every little critical thought I'd ever had about myself came at me, all at once. I wasn't good enough, not pretty enough, certainly not smart enough to see the truth. A man would never choose me exclusively, and I'd definitely die alone…" Violet sighs.

"Bullshit. Their betrayal says nothing about your worth and everything about them," I interject. I can see it so clearly, I don't understand why that asshole didn't. She's a treasure. I would give anything to make her happy. And she deserves so much more than anything I have to offer.

She smiles briefly, but it's not a happy smile. "After wallowing in self-pity for a while, I became more hardened. I tried to convince myself that I'd fallen into a trap, that love is for suckers and that I'd be better off on my own. I pretty much vowed to myself that I'd never be stupid enough to trust anyone like that again." She looks up at me again, and

I try very hard not to fall. Because her words hit me like daggers. *Love is for suckers. She'd be better off alone…*

"I understand," I whisper.

"I know. That's why we make such a good team, I think," she says.

Do we? What does that mean, anyway, a good team? Does she mean to continue our arrangement, or whatever this is? This boyfriend and girlfriend situation; it's nice and safe and good enough, until she finds what she really wants elsewhere?

"Now…" She takes a deep breath and squeezes my hand. "I've answered your question. Your turn to tell me something."

"What do you want to know?" I ask, but I can hardly hear my own voice over the hammering in my chest.

"What's going on with you? You've been acting weird since we got back."

I exhale sharply through my teeth.

"Perhaps I was even more unprepared for that surprise meeting than you were," I say.

Her eyes are wide with concern, but also, compassion, which encourages me to clarify.

"In the moment, everything was fine, I actually had a nice time at dinner. But now… I feel like an impostor. Like I don't belong."

"Chris, no!" Her grip on my hand tightens, and she scoots closer to me.

"You'd said it yourself on the train yesterday. That I could be your type, but with a few tweaks…" I whisper. "I figured out now what that means."

"I was trying to make a point. I didn't mean to imply—" she stammers.

"After seeing him… it all made sense. And as a result, I…"

She shakes her head.

"I wanted to hurt him. *Really* hurt him. For everything he did to you, but also, because—" I close my eyes and force myself to say the words. Because if I don't let it out, my chest might just explode. "I'm so fucking jealous, I don't know what to do with myself."

"Jealous? Of that asshole? That's ridiculous!" Violet argues.

Her reaction almost makes me recoil from her touch. It shouldn't surprise me, though. I'm trying to be honest and express myself, but it's unappreciated as usual. Coming from her, that hurts more than I could anticipate.

"Chris, please look at me," she says.

I shake my head. I literally can't. It's too painful.

"I'm so sorry, it seems I'm not expressing myself very well," she says.

Nice job, backpedaling. I'm not going to fall for it, though.

"When I saw him, I felt *nothing*. Well okay, I felt

anger and disdain. I didn't feel any sense of loss or heartache. I literally have no idea what I ever saw in him. That's why I mostly ignored him and went off on Joyce instead. He's a nobody, but she was supposed to be my friend. Still, she chose that idiot and his lies over our friendship."

I'm still shaking my head, still wringing my hands and failing to stay calm. I was better off in the damn bathroom earlier.

"I realized I never loved him. Not even when things were new and fresh and fun. At the time, I thought I did, but I didn't know what love felt like. I had no reference for it. Whereas now, I have the benefit of a new perspective."

What does that even mean? Why are we even still talking about any of this? Maybe I should check into a hotel, or something. Anything, just to get away from this feeling of defeat. We can talk about continuing our arrangement once I've calmed down. Or we could try being friends. Or I'll never see her again. I don't know which would be worse.

"Chris." She reaches for my shoulder, making my skin burn with an undeserved and unwanted yearning for her. It's too intense to bear.

"Stop, Violet."

"Chris, are you even hearing me?" she asks.

"Yeah. You didn't love him. Love is for suckers, right?" I counter.

"What? That's literally not what I'm trying to say!"

"Then?"

"I didn't know what love was back then, because I'd never really felt it before. That's why it was so easy to dismiss. But now, I know better, because I have."

I glance in her direction. A part of me expects to see the deceit in her eyes. Or at least a certain coldness, indicating that she's holding anything back. But much like literally every other time I've looked at her since yesterday, I just feel one thing. Yearning.

"I was trying to tell you after we got lunch, but then the bus came…" Her voice trails off.

"Tell me what?"

"That I love you."

It takes me a second to comprehend her words. Because they can't be true. This can't be happening. I don't belong with her. We're just playing boyfriend and girlfriend so she can feel whole again, but… I'm not that guy.

I'm not the guy who gets told: 'I love you.'

"Now don't go freaking out on me and running away," she whispers.

"What?" I stammer.

"You know, the same old story. Boy meets girl; girl falls for boy; boy gets cold feet as soon as the L-word is said," she says.

"That's a thing?" I don't know what's harder to believe. That guys run away in these types of situations, or her confessing her love for me. Both are ludicrous.

"Chris…" Violet's gray eyes plead at me to keep staring into them. There's so much promise there, hints of miracles I have yet to discover. "You're it. You're the one for me."

"Violet, how can you be so sure?" I wonder aloud.

"When you know, you know." She shrugs.

That's such a vague statement, it's almost meaningless. And yet it perfectly describes the state I've been stuck in since yesterday. Jesus. This is why I've been such a mess. Not over something as petty as performance anxiety, but because this has always been way more than a game of pretend for me.

"I don't have a frame of reference for *any* of this…" I suck in a deep breath through my teeth.

"I know. You don't have to say it back. You don't have to do anything. But I had to tell you, because it's been there on the tip of my tongue all afternoon…" she whispers.

"I love you too," I mouth.

Her lips part with a soft gasp. That's when I grab her. I grab her sweet, beautiful face and I kiss her like I should have done the moment we got back here. And she meets me halfway, pressing her mouth to mine, arching her body forward against me, burying her hands in my hair.

There's no time for hesitation or doubts, I just

follow my instinct and wrap one arm around her waist, guiding her back and pinning her against the sofa. I can manipulate her so effortlessly, I should have worried if she's really into it. If not for her hands rushing to pull my shirt out of the waistband of my jeans, then starting to caress my back underneath. All while kissing me so hungrily, I'm guaranteed to be wearing more lipstick now than she is.

Jesus Christ, this girl is amazing. *My* girl.

When you know, you know is exactly right. I know now. I love her. And she loves me. This is real. It's always been real, for her as well as for me.

CHAPTER SIXTEEN

* Violet *

Just how we got from having that excruciatingly tense conversation, to Chris pouncing on me for the most mind blowing kiss of my life so far, I'll never know. Words were said. Feelings were confessed. He loves me too. I can't believe it!

My heart is ready to explode with joy, and at the same time, his body, pressing me down into the sofa cushions, is fanning a much more primal desire, a lot further south. It's always been simmering under the surface, of course. Since last night, I've been desperate for his kisses. His touch. His body. I want him so badly, it consumes me, and as a result, I'm unable to pace myself any longer.

I don't wait to find out if he's okay with me taking his shirt off, I just start unbuttoning whatever part of it is in reach. Our only means of communication are moans and grunts, which are hardly enough to establish consent. Our body language tells me we're on the same page, though. He's tugging at my dress, which is a challenge as long as he's on top of me. And his manhood is prominently obvious as he grinds down against my thighs. Ah, it's so very close to where I need it, but I can't find it in me to try and stop him or direct him. He needs this, perhaps even more than I do.

When he opens his eyes and looks down at me, I see it so clearly. In between further breathless kisses, I can feel how impossible it has been for him to wait. And yet also how difficult it remains to continue.

He's torn between pleasure and worry, always with that expression on his face which seems to ask: 'Is this okay?'

"Chris, I want you," I breathe, while running my hand down his lower back and over his ass.

My man is rather blessed in this department too, and I can't resist and grab a handful. Who knew? Maybe size does matter. All I know is, he's damn sexy and I can't get enough of him.

He pushes back onto his elbows and looks down at himself and me. I quickly take the opportunity to wiggle out of my dress, before unbuttoning the rest of his shirt and pushing it back over his shoulders.

"You can breathe, right? I'm not too heavy for you?"

"You're perfect, Chris." I run my hand down his chest, across the patch of curly fuzz in the center and down his happy trail. So soft and pettable. I wouldn't change a thing about him. No tweaks required. Nothing. Not his belly, nor his love handles.

He flinches at every caress, but he doesn't stop

me.

"God, look how sexy you are!" I purr. "All this, just for me?"

I cup my hand over the bulge in his jeans and squeeze.

He shudders under my touch, closing his eyes.

"I still can't believe—" he speaks in bursts, trying but failing to catch a deep breath. "This is really happening?"

"Oh, it's happening!" I tell him, while unbuckling his belt and undoing the button of his jeans. "Show me everything…"

He shifts his weight to one side, and fumbles with his fly, letting his erection spring free. It's beautiful. Thick like the rest of him, and pointing straight at me like it knows exactly where it belongs: inside. I pull my panties aside and dip my fingers inside my pussy, coating them in my own wetness. Then I grab his cock, and his eyes roll back into his head, though I'm not even doing anything yet. He's so close, so desperate, just like me.

"I want to feel you in me."

He groans, and his hips start to tremble. "I won't be able… To hold back."

"I don't want you to hold back. Take me. I'm all yours!" I plead.

I spread myself wide just as he lowers himself down. I can just about guide him to the right place, before I'm forced to withdraw my hand. His head is pressing up against my entrance, working to spread my lips apart. I'm tight after all these months alone, and he's *big* big. But that doesn't worry me. The pressure is so delicious, I try to raise my hips to meet him.

My hands land on his ass, dragging him down into me, and with just the slightest wiggle, he's in and I cry out his name.

"Chris! Oh my God, don't stop!"

Although he's panting already, he keeps pushing down until he's buried deep inside me. There he rests, with his forehead against mine and urgent huffs tickling my lips.

"Shit, this feels… So good!"

"Sogood!" I repeat.

He surrounds me, overwhelms me. And by God, he smells so good!

My thighs are spread wide to accommodate him; legs flail, trying but failing to get around his waist and hook together. I try to make up for it with my hands, touching every part of him within reach. His skin is soft, even the scars. And the fact that he isn't chiseled like an underwear model makes me want to touch him even more. I didn't know it could feel like this. I didn't know I could want someone as much as I want him.

His eyes are shut, and his movements erratic. One

moment he's withdrawing, but not too far, then he pushes into me again, but just a little. It's just enough to drive me insane. Is he holding back for my sake or his?

"Chris, I need—" I gasp when he slams into me, his whole body tensing up, and his hips shuddering and grinding against my slick pussy. The length of his cock seems to tremble and convulse, and he's choking back a loud groan into the sofa cushion next to my head.

I try to move, to ride his wave of release towards my own, but he's so big and heavy on me, I'm helplessly stuck in this limbo. Too horny to back down, yet not quite where I need to be yet.

"I'm sorry," Chris whispers. "I couldn't make it last."

I wrap my arms around his neck, guiding his head in my direction so I can kiss him.

He moans against my lips, while twitching into me almost mindlessly. That's enough to push my excitement even higher. Fuck, I could kill for an orgasm right now. I know it's hard to come by, but it's all I can think of.

This is just our first time. His first time ever. I'm not going to let it be the last. We have all night, and then we have the rest of our lives to chase that elusive high…

CHAPTER SEVENTEEN

* Chris *

I should be embarrassed, blowing my load right at the start… Intellectually, I am. Practically, I can't muster the energy, because I've seemingly spilled it all into her.

The look in Violet's eyes is wild; she must be so disappointed in me. Hell, I would be too. I'd feel cheated. But then she grabs my face and pulls me down for a kiss, and by the magic of her sweet tongue, she brings me back to life.

I don't even realize when I start moving again, matching her rhythm with my hips until I feel myself growing harder again. Is this even possible? So soon?

Her pussy feels so wet and hot and perfect, I can't imagine ever pulling out. I don't want this moment to end, and seemingly, neither does my dick.

She's working hard to move underneath me. I can feel her little body wiggle and fight. Leaning up onto my elbows gives her more room. The effects are instant. Her hips try to match my pace, raising up and tilting to meet me, to take me in even deeper than I'd been before.

Jesus Christ. It's so good. I never imagined it like

this. Of all the lonely nights I've spent with just my right hand for company, I never once dreamed up an experience which comes close to this.

Her hungry kisses keep me coming back for more. Every so often, her eyes open to look at me. I feel so seen. So wanted. Dare I say it—loved?

This beautiful woman—more so with damp strands of hair sticking to her forehead and cheeks flushed and red—she's all mine. She's giving herself to me. She says she loves me.

I'd find it hard to believe, if not for the emotion welling up in her eyes. If not for how her body not just accommodates mine, but actively seeks me out. Because every time I withdraw, her eyes narrow anxiously, only to relax again when I bury myself in deep.

"Yes! Just like this!" she urges, when I speed up a little.

Holy shit, I'm not sure how long I can last this time. I shut my eyes and try to calm down. *You've already got a second chance; you're not getting a third one. Make it count!*

At first my movements were uncertain, but now I'm getting the hang of it. I raise myself up onto my left arm, hook my right under her knee for leverage, and settle into a new movement. In and out in smooth strokes, all the while admiring the jiggle in her cleavage that results.

She's gorgeous. Flawless alabaster skin as far as the eye can see, the black lace push up bra she's nearly spilling out of wrapped around her like a bow on a precious gift. Her face glistens with little beads of sweat, while her red shiny lips part with breathless moans. A picture so perfect, I couldn't have conjured it up in my wildest dreams. And as the icing on the cake, she smells like vanilla. My favorite.

Not only do I not deserve any of this, I look absolutely ridiculous. My new white shirt is now soaked and hanging around my shoulders almost like a damp cape. Sweat has continuously been dripping down my hairline and into my eyes and beard. And my jeans cling stubbornly to my thighs, ever since I carelessly shoved them down just far enough to free my cock.

With every thrust of my hips, I feel myself shudder. Excess flesh, countless scars, and stretch marks dancing as if to mock me. To remind me how wrong this is. She can't really want me. She's doing this out of pity!

"Chris," she whispers. "Chris!"

I meet her gaze and am stunned at what I see. That same hunger. That same admiration from before. "Where'd you go, Chris?"

I shake my head and try to focus on her again. I have to make it good for her. If I can give her even a fraction of the pleasure she's given me, perhaps I…

"Come back to me." She stretches her arms out at me, gesturing to lay down on top of her again. "I need to feel you."

Reluctantly, I lower myself until my belly squashes into her again. Our skin is cool and damp when it meets, but only for a second before heating up again. She caresses my beard, my hair, while guiding me down further until our lips meet. Shit, there's her tongue again, showing me all the same affection and need and hunger from before. As if she didn't see, or didn't realize, just how mismatched we are.

And I can't help but speed up, rutting against her like an animal in heat.

"Yeah, keep doing that!" she mumbles against my mouth. "Holy shit, Chris!"

Her hand travels down my back, caressing and fondling me. She grabs my side hard, angling her hips forward, which lets me in deeper. It's as if a red haze descends on me, blinding me to all those obvious truths I recognized only moments ago.

She needs this. I cannot give up. I've got to make it good… For her… For us.

Kisses turn to licks turn to muffled moans and nibbles. She's slipping, the surety in her movements waning, until she's twitching and whining and clawing at my back. And I'm exhausted, and I can't do much more than this, but I don't fucking stop even though my hips are trembling and the muscles in my thighs burn.

And then she goes rigid and digs her nails into my side, just as I slam into her with all I've got left. Her body clenches like a fist around my cock, holding me in place. Begging, squeezing, milking me until I come undone for the second time. Does she know?

God, how desperate am I?

For a brief moment there, I forgot myself. I got so swept up in the moment, in all those new sensations I was feeling , that I didn't think. Now, as I catch my breath, all the doubts come rushing back.

I'm too big and heavy for her; this must be uncomfortable. She tries to catch a breath and straighten out her leg, confirming my suspicion. I scramble onto my elbows again, trying to give her space.

"Don't go."

"I'm all sweaty and—" I stammer.

"So what? I'm sweaty too," she mumbles lazily, then plants a soft kiss on my lips.

It happened. We did it. My first and second time rolled into one. She told me she loved me and I lost it. I pretty much jumped her right there, and she caught me. This is becoming a pattern between us. Even when I thought I'd messed it up by finishing too soon, it was her kisses that brought me back. Is it always going to be like this? Am I always going to question and second-guess myself? Does it get easier?

"What were you thinking about?" she asks.

"Mhm?"

"You looked down at me, and your eyes just went kind of blank and distant. Like you weren't really into it anymore."

I stare at her, studying how her eyebrows pull together, forming a line in between. Oh shit, she thinks I was looking at *her* then?

"I…" The words evade me. How do I explain this without sounding pathetic?

Her eyes widen further, reminding me that I have to say *something* or else she'll think the worst.

"You looked so beautiful underneath me. Just like an angel. And I…" I say.

Although her expression calms slightly, she still looks concerned.

"Shit, I should have worn a condom, right? I didn't stop to think!"

She shakes her head and smiles. "I got tested, so I'm safe, and I already know you are…"

Safe… Yeah, I guess that's one word for it. Because as long as I'm around, I'd rather die than let any harm come to her. But what if I'm the one who's—

"Wanna know what I was thinking?" she asks.

I nod, grateful to take the easy way out.

"So, you straightened up, and grabbed my leg, and you were giving it to me good, like…" She bites her lip and bucks her hip up at me, which kind of tickles.

"And I thought about how lucky I am to have met you. How good you feel. How I want to keep doing this over and over… And it kind of kept building inside of me, and I just needed for you to not stop."

She smiles up at me. Radiant and sweet and naughty all at once.

"I'm sorry I couldn't go any longer," I tell her. "Next time, I'll—"

"I'm trying to tell you that you're the first guy to ever make me cum, and you're over here apologizing. What the hell, Chris!" she teases.

I stare at her. Into those deep gray eyes of hers. And all my worries and fears fade until I no longer remember any of them.

"What?"

"This was the first time, Chris. The first time I didn't have to fake it, or finish myself off later in secret. It's like our bodies… They just fit, you know?"

"That's a thing too? Guys just finish and leave you to manage your own orgasm?" I wonder aloud.

"I feel like I'm not doing myself any favors by telling you all the shit people do. Don't get any ideas, okay?" She grins.

"I would never." I rest my hand on her cheek and brush my thumb across her swollen bottom lip.

"I know."

"In fact, since I'm ahead, I owe you another one,"

I say. "It's only fair."

"I swear, if you utter the phrase 'tit for tat' right now, I'm going to knee you in the nuts."

I glance down at us, our sweaty naked bodies still mashed up against each other. This sight would have horrified me moments ago, but now it has taken on a new meaning. Our bodies fit, she says. They do, actually. They fit pretty well. "That would be logistically difficult, sweetheart."

She presses her lips together, but a grin breaks through, and shortly thereafter, a giggle. Her entire core seems to vibrate as she laughs, which sets her off even more.

Holy shit that tickles, which makes me laugh too. And as I do, a lightness settles in my chest which makes me realize, I'm not worried anymore. Nothing can come between us, certainly not all the petty worries that seemed like such a big deal earlier.

I made her cum. *I* did that. Shit. That's all I need, isn't it?

As long as I have this beautiful woman in my arms, as long as I can continue to make her smile and keep her happy, everything will be right in my world.

EPILOGUE

* Violet *

Three Months Later.

We didn't waste any time. After coming back from Edinburgh, Chris and I went straight to his place. Wrapped in a blissful haze of new love, we couldn't stand to be apart for more than a few minutes at a time. Luckily, he worked from home, and I didn't have any project to work on for the moment.

There wasn't a discussion about it, honestly. We just sort of moved in my stuff over the next week or so, and that was that. Luckily the lease on my flat was up anyway, so I could get out of that place, leaving the bad memory of finding Sam and Joyce together there behind. We've even adopted a cat, a red tabby named Cookie, who turns out to be even more in love with Chris than I am. And I couldn't be happier.

Of course, some adjustments needed to be made. I've had to get my messy tendencies under control, not leave a trail of sketches and paint all over the floor whenever inspiration strikes. And Chris started adopting healthier eating habits. I pretended not to notice, but the evidence of his old lifestyle was obvious the moment I walked in on that first day. As was his embarrassment, while he quickly tried to clear the empty takeout containers and energy drink cans off his desk, and out of his previously unused kitchen…

It's been easy, almost effortless, because we're doing it together. And we don't judge each other when we inevitably slip up. Still, one of my favorite times of the day is cooking dinner with him, simply because it's new for both of us. Previously I would buy a lot of pre-packaged salads or ready meals for one, but now we take turns picking new recipes to try, and have explored an entire world of flavors we never knew before. Maybe he *was* excited about expanding his palate before; he just never had the motivation to do it on his own. And he's become quite the baker, ever since trying out that first brownie recipe he found online…

As a result, he's even lost a little weight, whereas I've gained a little. It's cool, because we're doing a lot of *something else* as well, meaning we're both fitter than we've ever been. I'm glad we don't know too many of the neighbors, because I'm sure our bedtime antics must have made us the talk of the building. Even Cookie is quite fed up with it, giving me grumpy cat glares whenever we start kissing or cuddling. She's just jealous, because she wants Chris' undivided attention and will only get placated by treats and belly scratches after…

We might still be in the honeymoon period of our

relationship, but it's nothing like I've ever experienced before. This time, it won't be short-lived. This time, it won't all turn out to be an elaborate ruse or lie. This is real. This is for life. And I can't wait for the two of us to grow old together, still cooking dinner side by side, still curling up on the sofa to watch our favorite shows or movies. Still holding hands, every single time we go out, even if it's just to the nearest supermarket. And then heading home for a whole lot more…

Everything is great. I can't think of anything that would make our life together any better or more special.

"Violet! Come sit with me." Chris waves at me from the living room couch and pats the seat next to him. On the coffee table, there's a crisp white envelope with an unfamiliar logo in the corner. I hide my curiosity when I sit beside him, as close as I can possibly manage.

"Yes, babe. What's up?" I ask, resting my hand on his thigh.

Cookie jumps up into his lap, purring as soon as his hand settles on her. I'd be a little jealous, if they weren't so damn cute together. There's nothing more adorable and endearing than my big, burly boyfriend gently petting the cat, which looks comically small under his hand.

"Just got some news. Pretty big news." He eyes me

briefly, then stares at the letter on the table.

"What is it?"

"Just before Edinburgh, I'd applied for a different job. I made it through three rounds of interviews, but then they ended up choosing another candidate. They said they'd keep me in mind for any future openings, but with everything that's been going on, I never gave it a second thought…"

"Oh?"

"And now…" He nods at the letter.

"They've offered you a different position?" I ask, while taking his hand. "Is it still what you wanted?"

"It's… It's a huge step up for me, actually. But there's a catch." Chris picks up the envelope and stares at it for a moment, before making eye contact with me again. I can't quite read his expression. He's excited for sure, but there's also something else, something he's holding back.

"I wouldn't be working from home anymore. Well, not every day, anyway." His eyebrows pull together into a concerned frown.

I fold my leg up underneath myself and turn to face him. "It's nearby, though?"

Chris hesitates, his gaze shifting back to the letter. "Well… not exactly."

My heart skips a beat. "What do you mean?"

"The job is in Reading. It's a big promotion, and I could commute from here… But it won't be like now.

I would only be working from home once a week." His words hang in the air, heavy with unspoken worries.

Reading. It's close enough to stay here in Teddington, but it will still change the daily routine we've settled into these past few months. I search his eyes, hoping to understand what he's still not telling me.

"So… What do you want to do, Chris? Are you taking it?"

He pulls me closer, his thumb tracing gentle circles on my hand, but his eyes are full of uncertainty. "I don't know. I never thought I'd get an opportunity like this. It's the kind of job that could really set us up for the future… But there's something else I need to say first."

There's a heaviness in the air between us; it's making my heart beat faster. "What is it?"

Chris exhales sharply. His grip on my hand tightens as he begins to speak. "The day we met, on the train… I was such a mess, remember? But that didn't put you off or scare you away. You sat with me, talked to me, and even offered to tag along without even knowing a damn thing about me."

"Of course, I remember. Best decision I ever made." I lean into him, planting a soft kiss against his upper arm.

He swallows hard, his voice growing heavier.

"Violet, I never told you, but you saved my life that day. I was in such a dark place. Losing my dad, even though we'd fallen out of touch… It shook me to my core. He—he destroyed himself with alcohol, and I was so close to heading down the same path. But you… You caught me. You showed me that no matter my history, I could have a different outcome, a different future. I don't know where I'd be without you."

I reach up to cup his cheek. The tears welling up in my eyes make it hard for me to focus. I know how hard it is for him to express his feelings, at least the darker ones. I've of course had my suspicions about all this, but the fact that he's finally opening up and telling me directly means everything.

There's so much I want to say, but all I can manage is a soft: "Chris…"

He takes a shaky breath, his eyes locking onto mine with a fierce intensity. "I never imagined I'd feel anything like this. What we have… it's everything I didn't know I was missing. And I've never had the guts to properly thank you for everything you gave me that day, and every day since. The last thing I want is to jeopardize what we have now. If you'd rather we carry on like we have been these last three months, I'll gladly turn down the job. I don't want anything to come between us, Violet. I promised myself that I'd spend the rest of my life making you happy. So it's your decision."

I point at the letter, and he hands it to me. Giving it a quick read, I'm starting to understand his dilemma. It's a senior position in the company's IT department, and the money is life changing. We've had a wonderful time these past few months, but in the back of my mind, I knew we couldn't carry on like this. I'd have to get back to my work eventually too. You can't paint murals from home, so why should his job be any different?

My chest swells with love for him, and excitement for this opportunity he's been offered. I know he wants to accept, and it means so much to me that he's willing to sacrifice his career for my happiness. What he doesn't seem to realize is that his happiness is my happiness. This beautiful thing we share, it goes both ways. It always will.

Before I get the chance to speak up, he continues, his voice softer now, and cracking with emotion. "To show you how serious I am about us, about spending the rest of my life with you, I wanted to ask you something as well. I'd be lost without you, Violet. And I'm sorry I couldn't muster the courage to do this any sooner, Still… if you'll have me…"

He reaches into his pocket, pulling out a small velvet box. "Will you marry me?"

"Holy crap, Chris!" I'm trying like hell to blink the tears out of my eyes, and can barely find my voice.

"Yes… yes, of course I will!"

Chris lets out a breath he'd been holding, a wide grin spreading across his handsome face as he slips the sparkly diamond ring onto my finger. It fits perfectly, just like us. When the hell did he buy this? And how did he know exactly what I'd like?

"I love you, Violet," he whispers, his forehead resting against mine as his big, strong arms surround me. "Always will."

"I love you too, Chris," I reply, feeling once again like the luckiest girl in the world. "And nothing—not a job, nor anything else—could ever change that."

As we sit there, wrapped up in each other, with Cookie purring contentedly between us, I know deep in my heart that wherever we go, whatever happens, we're in this together. I knew it from the moment we met. At the time, I just didn't dare hope that my one night boyfriend would turn into my forever husband so soon. And I couldn't be happier.

I love him more than I ever thought I could love another person. And he loves me at least as much, if not more. This is it. All I've dreamed of. My very own viking teddy bear for life.

Maybe later, we'll start planning that wedding. Or maybe we'll just practice for the wedding night first. Because that's never going to change. He might start going to the office soon, but we'll still have our evenings and nights together. Our poor neighbors won't know what hit them.

When I press my lips to his, he reciprocates hungrily. I glide my hand across his broad chest and down the sexy curve of his belly. He sighs into my mouth when I reach the hem of his t-shirt and make contact with his bare skin underneath. The way his body seems to relax under my caresses now never fails to make me smile. It's a complete departure from those early times, when he would often flinch at first.

We've come so far together already. I can't wait to see what else is in store for us.

"Husband," I whisper, before plucking at his bottom lip with my teeth. "I love the sound of that."

He groans and grabs my ass, dragging me up and into his lap. Cookie jumps away to make room for me, and settles on the armrest of the sofa instead with a jealous scowl on her face.

"So do you, eh?" I tease, while slipping my hand into the waistband of his jeans and grabbing his thick cock.

"Always. Wife…" he growls.

Jesus, hearing him say that does things to my insides which I can't quite explain. Turns out, we won't be planning anything *later*. We're doing the whole wedding night and honeymoon and everything in between right now. Poor neighbors indeed.

AUTHOR'S NOTE

Thanks so much for reading *One Night Boyfriend!*

Perhaps you've been following me for a while, perhaps you're new to my work. But now that you're here, I'd like to give you a little background on how this book came to be...

My writing career started all the way back in October 2012 when I took a very deep breath, closed my eyes, crossed my fingers and even my toes and clicked 'Publish' on my first short story. That steamy little piece called *Ladies' Day*, and the book it grew into eventually ([Beautiful Stranger](#)) are still relevant today because it features a curvy heroine and her more mature lover. It serves as my first foray into steamy body positive romance.

Since then, I've published a whole bunch of books, in various romance sub genres; as L. Moone I write contemporary, and as Lorelei Moone I write about shifters, vampires and other paranormals. Certain themes tend to repeat themselves throughout my catalogue.

Beauty lies in the eye of the beholder. The hang-ups we tend to have about ourselves and our bodies often aren't shared by the opposite sex. While it's a lot more popular to write about gorgeous curvy ladies and muscular alpha males, I have a clear preference for the opposite: dad bod heroes and their admirers. I just never saw many of these books out there. Jessa Kane and her sexy big boy titles, *Hefty* and *Husky*, sparked a change in the romance landscape in 2020. I devoured those books and couldn't get enough. I'm seeing more and more authors enter this space, which is hugely exciting, because I've been writing about plus sized heroes for over ten years now! Finally, our time has come to make this niche more mainstream!

I first started writing *One Night Boyfriend* during a rather tumultuous period in my life, when I was travelling to attend a funeral. That first funeral was just the beginning, and eight months later, after finally publishing the book, we're at four funerals and counting within our close family/friend circle and quite a few more within our extended friend group. It's been a rough time, which I only knew how to deal with by escaping into my stories. Within quick succession, I finished and published *Blindly in Quarantine*, and *One Night Boyfriend*. Something tells me I've got at least another book or two in me before the end of 2024..

Things are still raw, and day-to-day life has changed forever as a result of the personal losses my husband and I incurred. Grief is a funny thing, which makes you react in weird, unpredictable ways. But hey, at least I'm putting out some of my best work so far (even if I say so myself). I hope you agree. :-)

But, enough of all that depressing stuff. For me, I think Chris is one of my favorite book boyfriends (though I feel like I say that about every single one of them). His chance meeting with Violet is the best possible thing that could have happened to him at the worst possible time in his life. Isn't that how things work out sometimes? You never know where you might end up months or sometimes even days in the future and sometimes, the darkest times lay the base for the closest bonds and friendships... At least that's what I've found this past year.

If you're like me and you just can't wait to read more Dad Bod Romance, you'll be pleased to know that in addition to the *Husky Ever After* series, which *One Night Boyfriend* is a part of, you can also check out the now completed *Husky Men do It Better* series. There's also a similarly themed and very similarly named title from another series you might want to read, called One Night Stand. Yes, I might be slightly obsessed with the idea of casual hookups turning into so much more... ;-)

And that's enough from me. I hope you enjoyed the story as much as I did while writing it.

x, Lorelei

FIND ME AT:

- ❖ LMoone.com
- ❖ Lorelei Moone on Facebook
- ❖ AuthorLMoone on Instagram

I also write Paranormal Romance as Lorelei Moone. Check out LoreleiMoone.com for more information.

SPECIAL OFFER!

For a limited time, all new mailing list subscribers will receive a FREE short story, called At First Sight.

Claim your free copy here:

LMoone.com
**Look for the newsletter sign-up form at the
bottom of the page.**